BELIEVE ME

Paula Nicolson

Fireside Press

To Derry Nicolson

CONTENTS

Title Page	1
Copyright	2
Dedication	3
Believe Me	11
Prologue	12
Chapter 1	15
Chapter 2	18
Chapter 3	24
Chapter 4	30
Chapter 5	34
Chapter 6	39
Chapter 7	45
Chapter 8	50
Chapter 9	52
Chapter 10	54
Chapter 11	59
Chapter 12	62
Chapter 13	65
Chapter 14	69
Chapter 15	71

Chapter 16   75

Chapter 17   78

Chapter 18   83

Chapter 19   88

Chapter 20   91

Chapter 21   96

Chapter 22   102

Chapter 23   106

Chapter 24   110

Chapter 25   117

Chapter 26   122

Chapter 27   128

Chapter 28   133

Chapter 29   139

Chapter 30   141

Chapter 31   145

Chapter 32   147

Chapter 33   151

Chapter 34   157

Chapter 35   160

Chapter 36   163

Chapter 37   167

Chapter 38   170

Chapter 39   178

Chapter 40   182

Chapter 41   188

Chapter 42   192

Chapter 43   199

Chapter 44   202

Chapter 45   204

Chapter 46   207

Chapter 47   212

Chapter 48   214

Chapter 49   219

Chapter 50   224

Chapter 51   229

Chapter 52   231

Chapter 53   236

Chapter 54   242

Chapter 55   247

Chapter 56   251

Chapter 57   255

Epilogue   263

Praise For Author   265

Books By This Author   267

Acknowledgements   269

BELIEVE ME

A
Dr. Nancy Strong Novel (1)

By

Paula Nicolson

PROLOGUE

1995

She lifted her head.

It hurt. She lay on her stomach. She was stretched out on the floor. She could still move. She could breathe. She concentrated on breathing. Raising her throbbing head slightly she spotted two wine glasses and an empty wine bottle. On the floor. At the foot of the sofa. She remembered. They had been drinking. Red wine. One glass had a lipstick stain. Hers. She recognized the shade. She raised herself with all the strength her arms could muster.

There now. Gently. Keep steady. You can do it.

Then suddenly, as if her body was being pierced by steel, her legs were wrenched apart and she felt she were being ripped in two.

'You bloody love it don't you?' And then a moan.

Of desire? No!

The pain became more intense. It no longer had any direction. The pain was all of *her*. There was nothing but pain. Two large hands pulled her over onto her back. Now she could see him. He pulled at her skirt. There was almost no need. It was already above her waist. But he smiled as he did so. He looked at her. His trousers were down below his hips and he descended into her. Again.

Should I scream? I don't think I can.

She wanted to faint. She felt her body shaking beyond her control. She could almost taste the wine on his breath. But also something rancid. Her senses swirled around but her brain was determined to stay alert. At least enough for her to experience the agony. And fear. She realized she was terrified. She knew she was helpless. This was something that she had never known before.

The only thing I can do is try to recall everything. Never forget. Never let him get away with this.

She was angry now, enraged, but sensed that she needed to hide it. She had to let him finish. He had to go. But it went on and on. She could see his large, long head. His dark empty eyes staring at her. His rough stubbled chin. Her strength dissolved from the pain and effort not to scream. She felt like a rag doll. And then it was over. Or that part was over. He collapsed on top of her, catching his breath. And then he kissed her. On her lips. No passion simply a shadow of a lover's affection. Her stomach wretched. She could taste the bile.

Should I smile? Will that make him bloody go?

Slowly he raised himself off her. He stretched his back grimacing slightly as if it had surprised him with a stab of pain. He stumbled a little, falling back with his full weight onto her legs. They hurt. She watched him. He was no longer interested in her. His energy went into moving, standing, pulling up his trousers. Zipping them up. Adjusting his shirt.

What now?

He moved toward the door of her living room and into the hallway. She tried to think.

Should I get up? See him out? Pretend not to notice him? That this was normal? What?

Imperceptibly there was a gentle knocking at the front door of her apartment.

'Ok. Wait'.

What the fuck? Is there someone else here?

Fear started to grip her once again. There could be others. Waiting. For me. Her breathing came in short gasps. She tried to keep them quiet. Almost a panic attack. The front door opened. Closed. She waited. Petrified. Then nothing. He had gone. *They* had gone.

✻ ✻ ✻

CHAPTER 1

2017

Dan opened the bedroom door balancing two mugs of tea in his right hand along with the morning mail in the other.

Anna raised herself up onto her pillows and smiled. It was the start of the Autumn Term. They both needed to get out of bed. Anna first as she had the commute. Dan pulled the blinds open blinking in the still-bright late September morning and looked at the envelopes in his hand dividing them into his and hers before climbing back into bed to drink the tea and read his post.

'That's odd' Anna remarked and passed an envelope over to Dan. 'Look at this'.

Inside the typed addressed envelope was a postcard with the words: *Looking forward to our next meeting my dear Anna.*

'What on earth does that mean?'

Dan looked at the words and shook his head 'Is there anything you want to tell me Anna?' he laughed. 'I would imagine it was a student. Perhaps a prank. Perhaps also an admirer. I bet you have a few don't you?'

'Oh, I don't know'. She suddenly felt weary. She loved her job but over recent years the numbers of students who wanted to study psychology had grown exponentially. There was less time than ever for research even though the university demanded their academic staff did more of it. There was no longer much time to get to know any student either.

'Best get up. Is Alison out of bed yet?'

'Doubt it' said Dan. 'It's your turn to chase'.

Alison their oldest child was 17. Doing her A levels and going through adolescent angst. Not a good combination.

'Alison! Are you awake?'

'Nearly' came the reply and both Dan and Anna laughed.

'OK I will chase. You do the boys'.

Robert and Anthony were their 14-year-old twins. Kind, happy, uncomplicated and already helping themselves to cereal and toast. Soon after, Alison joined them all in the kitchen, snapping at her brothers and pushing them out of the way as she grappled with her special vegan cereal hidden at the back of the cupboard.

Anna sighed and left them all to it. They were all becoming independent now and had less need of her intervention. At least once they were out of bed. Now she returned to her own preparations for the term.

She was still thrilled to have been appointed Professor of Social Psychology and Gender at the well-respected University of South East London, even though it meant a 40-minute train journey from their home in the leafy suburb of Endlesham.

Well the walk to the station is good for me.

She looked in the mirror noting that one or two white hairs could be seen curling themselves within the dark red mass of ringlets that, she had to admit, could make her look quite scary if she chose. Her dark green eyes complemented that east European appearance although she had no reason to believe that any of her ancestors had come from anywhere further than East Grinstead. She stepped into the shower emerging 10 minutes later wrapped in a large blue towel. She dried herself, put on her plain black trousers and white blouse, before moving quickly down the stairs. Kissing Dan and the children she grabbed her leather jacket, prized on her black boots and headed down the drive for the 10-minute walk to catch her train.

BELIEVE ME

✳ ✳ ✳

CHAPTER 2

'Here Anna!'

It was Gabriel Watson her head of department. He lived in the village beyond Anna's suburb and often tried to save her a seat on the train.

I bet he pisses people off with his case, coat, laptop taking up two places. We are far too polite in this country.

She was grateful though and pleased to see him. He was a sensible, generous boss who wanted everyone to feel involved in departmental decisions. Even so, not all of her colleagues were equally generous, and she was aware of several different plots to darken his reputation. As with many academics there were vicious rivalries in the scrabble for research grants, prestigious publications, promotions and attracting the best doctoral students. Department heads had discretion and power which some of them abused. But not Gabriel.

'What news? Anything going to happen this term?'

'Did you hear that Adrian Hanlon is to take early retirement? The university Council is wanting us to appoint a new Vice Chancellor asap'.

'Really? I knew he was being hounded by the press about his bloody enormous salary. Is that the reason?'

'Who knows? Anyway, you'll be over the moon to hear that I have listed you as one of the senior staff to be involved in the new VC's appointment panel'.

'Um. Ta very much. I think'.

Gabriel laughed. 'We all get to see the applications later today and then the short-listing begins'.

'Any women I wonder?'

'Possible. Don't know much yet'.

They both settled down in their seats. She noticed that Gabriel looked tired, despite recent weeks without the daily grind of meetings, budgets and students. There was even less hair on his shiny round head now, she thought, and he had definitely put on weight.

The price of management responsibility!

She was glad she didn't have any. Anna was now being jostled by the passengers standing in the aisle. A case banged into her face. The buckle of a handbag became caught in her hair. They arrived at Clapham Junction, apparently one of the busiest stations in the world. The torrent of passengers leaving and embarking always fascinated her. But then she thought she recognized someone. A man. In his early 30s. Blond hair with black streaks standing up on top if his head. He was getting off the train.

A former student of mine? Not sure. A bit old for that. Who is it? I guess he just reminds me of someone.

Her mind drifted towards the arrangements for the day ahead, although she now had to move things around if she were to take her place on the VC appointment committee. She then recalled the strange postcard she had received earlier that day and was just about to mention it to Gabriel when she saw that he was waving to the man with the spiky hair who seemed to be struggling to remain upright among the crowd of commuters heading down the steps.

That's it then. Must be a student. My brain is not firing on all cylinders yet. Early days.

They pulled into London Waterloo, moving with the tide of fellow travellers towards the vaulted exit, down the steps, through the tunnel to embark on the 10-minute walk to their campus - or at least the grand buildings set around a courtyard that comprised part of the University of South East London affectionately known as USEL. Other sites were in Dulwich and Bermondsey. Anna rarely had to go beyond the Lambeth site for which she was grateful.

By the time they had arrived at the main university entrance a deluge of others - colleagues and students, accompanied them. Excited chatter filled her ears. The young people surrounding her bringing back some of the many pleasures of academic life. Psychology was an especially popular discipline and rarely did their students present excessive difficulties to the lecturers because their department could select from the best and the keenest.

Gabriel nodded his goodbye 'I'll let you know the timing for this afternoon. See you later Anna'.

She wondered what made him choose her for this dubious honour.

Maybe they do want to appoint a woman. That'd be great.

She groped in her case, found her keys and entered her office. There was a smell of recently applied polish on the desk and chairs, although the window was grimy with only a dim light filtering through the sticky dust. She turned on her computer. Although she hadn't been near her office for the past 2 months she had been working hard on her latest book. It was about sexual harassment at work among high level professional staff such as doctors, finance executives and academics. She had had a substantial research grant enabling her to employ two enthusiastic post-doctoral researchers to interview men and women across these professions. Their findings were depressing.

Even in the 21st Century it seemed that women could not guarantee professional equality, and many considered their everyday working lives to be unpalatable or even dangerous in some cases.

Anna opened her emails, sighed before venturing down the corridor to fill the jug of her coffee maker in the landing kitchen.

Nothing of note. Just a boring list of admin responses needed.

Her return to the office was shortly followed by the balding head and the thick spectacles of Donald Delaney peering round the door. He wore a bright smile and bore an empty coffee mug. He gestured silently towards the coffee machine which had already begun to fill its jug with the warm aroma of fresh caffeine.

Thank God for that. It's Donald.

He was Professor of Criminal Psychology – and everyone really liked him. Including Anna. He sat down heavily on the chair next to her desk.

'You've heard the news then? About Adrian Hanlon?' She nodded.

'Well let's hope we can choose a cheaper and more effective VC this week'. They both laughed and Donald then proceeded to recount a list of Hanlon's transgressions entertaining Anna with accurate impressions of the retiring VC and members of his senior team. She was glad to be back at work and to have such brilliant colleagues to keep her sane.

Another person knocked on Anna's office door. A wild mop of reddish-brown hair appeared through the half open door followed by a whoop and their colleague Ellie Hart burst in. She grabbed Donald, hugging him tightly, laughing and then pounced on Anna.

'Hey so good to see you both again. What do you think of the news?'

'Adrian you mean?'

'I do. Indeed. Good bloody riddance eh?'

Well we need to be careful what we wish for.

But Anna kept those thoughts to herself. She felt relaxed and safe in her friends' company.

Safe. I've not thought about that for so long. But yes. Safe.

She smiled as she listened to Ellie and Donald exchanging news about their vacations but also, slightly more dangerously, about the papers and grant applications they had completed during the summer recess. However fond you were of your colleagues the environment could be competitive which sometimes lead to bitter rivalry.

Another thump on the door and Sandy Scott, the departmental administrator and assistant to the head of department, Gabriel, entered holding a large file which he placed on Anna's desk grinning at her as he did so.

'You are the chosen one! LOL. Make sure you appoint the right one'. Anna felt a chill enter the room which surprised her, although it soon passed.

'Are you on the selection panel then?' asked Donald and she couldn't help seeing Ellie watching closely for the answer.

'Not just the panel' Sandy interjected. 'The full works.'

Administrators know everything.

'What? What are you talking about?' Anna felt an increasing tension in herself and in the room.

'So. Short-listing meeting this afternoon, preliminary interviews Thursday morning, lunch with the university Council after that, and then dinner at the King William Hotel and formal interviews Friday morning.'

'Jesus'.

'Yup that's who we're looking for'. And with that Sandy left the room.

'Dark horse' said Donald and rose from his chair carrying his still half-full mug of coffee. 'Let us know how it goes. See you later'. He went out the door smiling, but Anna saw that the warmth was mostly directed at Ellie.

'What the Hell do you think you're doing agreeing to take part in that charade?' Ellie asked her. Ellie was Anna's closest friend both in the department and occasionally outside work.

'Look I only know what Gabriel told me on the train this morning. The head of department's decision. That I was to be on the panel. I'm beginning to think I have been sold a pup without even paying, if you see what I mean?'

Ellie laughed. 'I'd better go. Good luck. But I think you saw it too - that Donald is pissed off. He thought he was the favour-ite until just now'.

Anna was grateful to be alone now. She sighed and turned back to her list of awaiting emails. She scanned through to see if any of them would be relevant for the day ahead. Messages from students, timetable and room changes, special meetings were all there most of which had gone immediately into her electronic diary.

I sometimes think I am run by this bloody machine.

The only essential diary entry for the day though was the 2pm short-listing meeting in the Registrar's room on the ground floor. Then the morning was to begin with the new 2nd year seminar group of excited and anxious students who had passed their 1st year exams.

✻ ✻ ✻

CHAPTER 3

Monday after lunch

Anna and her colleague John Jones, who lectured on economic psychology, had decided to leave the university buildings to pick up some lunch-time sandwiches from a bar near Waterloo station.

Anna was hungry but also wanted to get away from the campus, which has suddenly become oppressive, for a while.

The sun was out and still warm. The streets were filled with students – indeed everywhere seemed to be overtaken by students today.

I guess it is the start of the new academic year. You get used to their absence and then they're back with a vengeance.

It was fun being with John who had absolutely no ambition to climb the greasy, electrified, academic pole.

He had left his 60th birthday some way behind after spending much of his career marrying and divorcing former students, several of whom shared children with him. He was a happy man and at long last had managed to form a lasting affectionate relationship with a woman of his own age who worked in the theatre with no interest in university politics.

John recognized the political risks of standing out from the crowd at work and not for the first time warned Anna that there were other things in life than career.

'I took a back seat when the kids were young – it seems my time now. The time for other women too'.

'Yeah, I get it. But you can still enjoy the students and write the occasional book. But being on that appointment committee! That's kind of asking to be noticed by those who might come to love you and those who will begin to hate you. And there are more of the latter believe me'.

She acknowledged the dilemma but felt she was being swept up into the professional foreground without any of her own maneuvering.

'I beg you to take the John Jones option!' he laughed. She smiled and for the umpteenth time that day gave a bewildered sigh.

What shall I do?

The pair returned to their offices discussing the meaning of success and happiness and to eat their sandwiches. As they entered the building, they bumped into Gabriel who beckoned Anna towards him requesting that they meet briefly before going into the short-listing meeting. She had a sense that something strange was happening but attributed it to the start of term and the end of a relaxing summer.

'There's something I want to talk over with you. It's a bit delicate'.

Intrigued she nodded, smiled over her shoulder at John, and followed Gabriel into his office. They both flopped into a couple of worn easy chairs with a relaxed familiarity.

'It's delicate and a bit embarrassing.' Anna nodded at him to continue.

'Well. Oh - damn it I'll just tell you now. Shirley Collins had a long affair with one of the candidates who is, I'm told, the chair of Council's favourite'.

'Two things. How do you know? And how is it we're the short-listing committee and there is a favourite already before we've even seen the CVs?'

'That's how it's done. You know that.' Gabriel smiled sadly.

'But – what to say or do about Shirley Collins? This could prove difficult as her case for promotion to a readership is about to be set before the Promotions Committee in the Autumn and he will ...'

'Or she!'

'Yeah. Likely'.

Anna was despondent and sensed that Gabriel felt similarly. Shirley Collins, a lecturer in psychological development, was not one of Anna's favourite people. Nor was Gabriel particularly keen. Shirley never took on her share of the departmental work-load and would burst into tears and cry 'racism' at the earliest opportunity. Her grandmother had originally come to London from Jamaica. A talented, and eventually wealthy, woman who had made sure her grandchildren had had the most expensive educations and a range of privileges that few others in the department had experienced. That did not prevent Shirley claiming that she was multiply disadvantaged.

'I am a woman and I am Black'. Most colleagues left her alone as much as possible as there was a strong chance that she would launch some kind of grievance against anyone who irritated her. The current system, with its emphasis on equality and diversity, indicated that she would win. So, the news of this affair with a potential VC was a particularly unexpected and unwelcome piece of gossip.

'Well I guess it doesn't particularly impact on the department does it? Not if this ex-bloke of hers impresses.' Gabriel nodded although didn't appear too convinced.

'Time to go. Ready?' He said. And they headed off to the ground floor and the Registrar's rather grand meeting room.

The clink of tea cups and mostly male voices greeted them as they pushed open the door. The room with its Victorian facade had been refurbished and was a beautifully preserved 19th Century dining room. A long, highly polished, table had been set by the Human Resources and catering staff with a pile of CVs, bottles of water, tumblers, pens, pencils and plates of biscuits placed at intervals along the centre. The French doors, adjoining a secluded quadrangle, were open allowing the warmth and brightness of the afternoon to infect the mood of the 12 men standing around the catering trolley grabbing cups of tea from a lone woman, Jennie, everyone's favourite member of the catering staff because she always produced the finest biscuits. And lots of them.

Gabriel and Anna took their cups of tea from the catering trolley. Roland Day, head of research, called the group to order. He sat at one end of the table and Jerry Middlemass, the Registrar, head of all the university administration, whose meeting room it really was, sat at the far end shuffling piles of papers and clearing his throat. The door opened and Joanna from 'HR' – the recently designated Human Resources department that had always been known as Personnel' as far as Anna remembered - entered.

That was a far better description – what on earth is a Human Resource?

Joanna's notepad and iPad at the ready. Her role was to ensure fair play and answer questions on procedure. At least that was what they had been officially told. Even so there was scarcely any evidence that HR did much beyond taking notes and nodding 'yes' whenever the VC or their stand-in posed a dilemma.

Anna and Gabriel sat next to each other and, as instructed, everyone began scanning the CVs.

'Do try not to confer' Roland reprimanded two professors from the Maths department both of whom glanced at him and then each other before continuing to share their comments on the CVs before them. Anna always found herself bemused by the types of things that potential VCs claimed to have done. The first candidate had apparently cycled from Land's End to John O'Groats.

Why would he want us to know that? It suggests his efforts are directed somewhere other than higher education.

Several applicants held community posts – chair of hospital trusts or on the boards of charities. Almost all, to Anna's mind, showed little concern with their own academic pathways which indicated they might fail to appreciate and nurture the work of the more junior members of staff if appointed. Those thoughts stayed with her until she arrived at Professor Marion Penny's CV. The first application that she had seen from a woman. This woman had not only held similar posts to the other applicants but secured and managed large grants and published her research.

Refreshing. An academic at last!

Anna felt slightly more optimistic. Marion was the first potential leader in her view. As she smiled intending to move onto the next batch of papers, she became aware of muttering around the table as well as exasperated sighs, particularly loudly from Gabriel as well as the maths professors. Clearly Roland had given up trying to prevent people conferring – but that was pointless anyway. To Anna, Marion was the only contender so far. She placed that CV to one side leaving the ones she had already seen face down next to the diminishing number she had read until then.

At that point Jennie, the 'tea lady', clattered into the room once again with fresh pots of tea, and 'yes!' more biscuits. All her previous offerings had disappeared leaving very few crumbs. The committee were clearly needing the calories and the comfort. Even Roland beamed at Jennie as he leaned back in his chair.

'A ten-minute tea and comfort break chaps' and he dashed out the room. Too soon he brought the room back to order. Most people continued to munch while crumbs fell onto the papers along the table and would doubtless eventually be filed among the unsuccessful candidates' applications in the vaults of the HR department until the official time for shredding.

Somewhat refreshed after the comfort break Anna moved to the next set of papers. She realized she was bored.

John's right of course. This is ludicrous and I really don't belong here among these people. It's going to be the John Jones option from now on. Keep your head down and enjoy what you have.

And her mind wandered to the new play at the Hampstead Theatre that she wanted to see. Jennie went around the table offering the last of the pot and Anna held out her cup smiling happily at Jennie. She felt free from pointless ambition at last.

So, who's next?

She paused and stared in disbelief at the paper before her.

'Professor Simon William Heath. Application for the post of Vice Chancellor of the University of South East London'.

She stared. She felt faint. The cup in her hand shook so violently that she spilt much of what was left over the papers on the table in front of her. Her head hurt and she shivered as the perspiration cooled down as rapidly as it had emerged.

Gabriel, seemingly unaware of her state nudged her. 'That's the bugger that Shirley Collins was bonking'. He sniggered, turned to look at Anna managing to rescue the half empty cup, putting his other arm around her to prevent her collapsing. A hushed silence hit the room and all eyes were on Gabriel and Anna caught in their strange embrace.

❋ ❋ ❋

CHAPTER 4

Anna had never felt quite as foolish as she did by the time she came out of her swoon.

What the frigg? What happened?

As with the majority of academics no-one knew what to do when someone was in distress of any kind, so it was little surprise that she awoke to find the kind, pink face of Jennie offering hot sweet tea and Joanna from HR proposing that the room had been too warm for so many people to work in. Although she kept repeating, mostly to herself, that the French doors had been open so there had been no need for anyone to faint.

'There should have been adequate ventilation for you all'.

Anna groaned inwardly. She hated sweet tea, but really liked Jennie so she tried to drink it gracefully. She smiled wanly at Joanna, whom she sensed was beginning to panic about health and safety issues. Joanna, like Jennie, was also a kind woman, the sort you could tell your troubles to when she wasn't panicking about regulations. Anna always got the impression that Joanna would rather be in the university counselling service than HR. HR were the people who would dissemble to carry out the will of frequently malicious senior staff regardless of any moral compass.

Anna recovered her composure. It took very little time for her to recall the cause of her demise.

Simon Heath. Christ. No way must it be him.

'Joanna, I need to be back in that meeting. Immediately. Please let them know and I'll come after you'.

'Don't worry' Joanna looked rather shocked. 'It's finished now. Only one candidate was shortlisted. Um – let me see – yes - Professor Heath – University of Littlehampton. Yes, that is the man. We're inviting him for interview'

'No!'

'It's OK Anna. You are on the list for the panel. And the candidate dinner of course. You have plenty more opportunities to add your opinion'. Joanna nodded affirmation towards Anna assuming she would be reassured but was aghast to see the colour drain out of her face. At that point Jennie slipped away with the tea trolley and Anna was dimly aware of its receding clatter.

'Are you OK Anna. Er, Professor Brosnan'. Joanna suddenly looked embarrassed and worn. To Anna's eyes her hair suddenly appeared grey and her face more lined than previously. *Joanna looks frightened. Why?*

'Can we talk? Privately?' Anna felt her throat tighten.

Can I actually tell her? I have to! I have to!

'Well' Joanna pulled herself to her full height and gradually retained some of her relative youth and energy.

'Of course. But I don't have my diary here. If you think you'll be Ok now I'll email you some available times to see if they are convenient.' Anna didn't feel happy about that arrangement but could tell it was the best she could get for now.

And will I have the strength to tell her anyway? I must! the man is a criminal.

'Are you sure you're OK now? Joanna was walking away as she asked, and Anna nodded.

I shall tell Ellie. I have to tell someone.

With that resolved Anna walked along the corridor, out and across the quadrangle where in the distance she saw the windows of the Psychology Department's offices and Ellie's head staring at her computer screen. She straightened herself, moved swiftly up the stone stairs towards Ellie's office.

'Hey what's up? You look as if you've seen a ghost. Are you OK?'

'No. I just passed out – during the short-listing meeting'

'Bloody Hell. What happened? You're not pregnant are you?'

At least it made them both snigger. Anna summoned up her strength to tell Ellie what had really happened. Just then there was a knock at the door.

'*Zut alors*. Come in.' But there was no need to issue the invitation because Donald Delaney was half way through the door.

'What on earth is the matter with you two? Chins up – I've got some gossip. Hot off the press'.

Both women stared at him.

'Well don't you want to know? 'He paused and looked at each in turn.

'I don't care I shall tell you anyway. Well the only short-listed candidate, Simon Heath sociology aficionado from Littlehampton University – he is a very old friend of mine and has already promised to develop our department and ensure research funding for social psychology and criminology.'

Donald, never Don for some reason, looked from one to another.

He's expecting a whoop of joy. What can I say now? A friend? That man?

'Well that sounds good' Ellie didn't sound particularly overjoyed, but Donald carried on regardless.

'Yeh. The man is ace. But – you'll never guess. He's been bonking that stupid cow Shirley. For years I'm told'.

'How on earth do you know all this?' from Ellie. Donald winked and tapped his nose.

'For you to discover for yourself. I'm told he is one for the ladies.' Anna was convinced that Donald had given her a wry look.

Does he think I'm interested in that type of man? Ugh. This has to be a bad dream.

'I need to go now. I have to speak to Joanna from HR. She's about to call me. See you both later'. Anna didn't think she could reach the door of Ellie's room without shaking but she managed it and walked past the 3 other doors to the safety of her office.

God. I need to process all this. What is going on? Donald knows that creep? They've been in touch already? And how the frigg does he know about Shirley?

Anna's computer pinged and an email from Joanna arrived suggesting a few possible meetings. Anna chose the first one suggested. She just had to let the appointment committee know what kind of man Heath was before Thursday.

❋ ❋ ❋

CHAPTER 5

There was a knock on the office door.

She could hear voices. Laughter. Her heart started pounding. Anna looked at her watch and realized it was her seminar group. She had totally forgotten them.

'Come on in' she shouted and a group of seven young women of different sizes and shades of brown and pink occupied all remaining available space.

'Hi Prof Brosnan' went the chorus.

'Come in, sit down and lovely to see you all too' and she meant it. The door then opened slowly and a young man with dreadlocks peered slowly into the room.

'And you Clayton. Great to see you too'. He grinned and sat down next to Anna facing the young women who were at various stages of grappling with their bags and cases pulling out notes and pens. Clayton didn't have a case or any previous notes. He seemed to rely on others' good will.

'Marge – let me have some paper.' She did. They then settled down to discuss leadership and gender issues. One of the women, Angie, was particularly concerned to know whether female biology prevented women's logical thought. Clayton railed against that view. The others backed him up. Anna, enjoying their efforts and enthusiasm lost herself in their company for the next 50 minutes. In the end everyone agreed that women might prove to be more effective leaders than men.

'They have more *emotional* intelligence don't they?' Wendy

summed up the group's arguments.

'Time for your statistics lecture guys' and they groaned, once again wrestling with their papers and bags, scraping back their chairs and leaving Anna's office. The room felt stale and too subdued after they had left. Slightly depressed. The corridor seemed quieter than usual too. Anna settled down to make a few notes to assist in her conversation with HR scheduled for later that afternoon. Her mind returned to everything that had happened to make this necessary.

20 years ago. I feel sick. Still. And unclean. How dare he do that to me.

Acknowledging her own anger made her feel slightly better. She had hated herself for years. Even after she and Dan had got together. Even after Alison was born. She had felt polluted. Degraded somehow. She had never been able to face telling Dan what had happened to her. She knew if she were to do so he would be on her side. He always was. But she also knew that he would try to dissect the 'evidence' of what had happened that night. That perhaps Simon Heath, her rapist had misunderstood what she had wanted? That maybe he wasn't a vile low-life but an inexperienced, awkward idiot. Dan always tried to be reasonable. He would never truly understand how wretched and guilty she felt herself to be.

That shouldn't be. I did nothing wrong.

But had she? She knew she had flirted with that man. He was her doctoral studies supervisor. She was young. Her friends were young. They all fancied him. Mostly because he had power. She understood that now. He was young – probably only 5 years or so older than most of them. It was he who introduced most of them to feminist critiques in the social sciences.

What a bloody joke.

She had felt so wonderful when he accepted her invitation to come home with her that evening. Her flat-mate was going home for the weekend. Her friends had dared her to invite 'the lovely Simon' as they called him, out for a drink.

Then but not now. He is vile.

She couldn't bear to think about this any further. But she had to do something. It was hard to think it, to form the words to describe what had happened. But he had *raped* her. Not just sex. It didn't seem like desire. He had hurt her. He had threatened her. He had told her she was a tease and was getting what she deserved. She realized now that her body was shaking. If she didn't get herself together now, she would lapse into uncontrollable sobs. I have to stop this man coming here.

She touched her keyboard. Almost as a means of distraction. A series of pings notified the arrival of several emails. She looked, particularly for anything from Joanna or related to the selection of the new VC. She sat back in horror as she looked down the list. **Simon@Little.ac.uk** had sent her a message.

Try to look. Try to be calm. He is worried. Now.

She opened the email. '*I am so looking forward to being with you. I gather we are all going to dinner on Thursday night. I can't wait*'.

OK. Now I have to call Joanna. It's urgent and this is evidence.

Anna reached across her desk for the phone just as her office door was vigorously pushed open. 'Hello Anna'. It was Shirley.

Had she really been Simon's lover?

She had always seemed so prim and proper. Butter wouldn't melt. Most colleagues acquiesced to this image complementing the belief that she was untouchable because of her apparent heritage, one that she used to protect her offensive idle nature. But she was hoping for promotion to a readership – where you took a lead on research. Shirley hardly did any.

'Anna. Can you advise me please?'

'Anna looked at her. As usual Shirley's face was passive with a barely perceptible smile hovered behind the mask, making her appear innocent and vulnerable.

'If I can Shirley. Of course.' Shirley was constantly asking for advice or favours from Anna, and maybe others too. So the conversation seemed commonplace - almost relaxing. Anna looked at Shirley. She sat back slightly in her chair, held her hands together as if she were a therapist. Shirley responded.

'I understand that an old boyfriend of mine might be coming to work here. In this university'.

'Oh?' from Anna.

'Yes. We were going to get married you know?' Anna's eyebrows shot up involuntarily, forcing her to try to calm her face down to its usual passive state when in Shirley's presence. Anna felt her heart thumping as she tried to suppress her personal physical encounter with Heath, while she prayed her distress remained invisible. Shirley was so manipulative that if she sensed any slight emotion or anything unusual, she would file it into her venomous brain to use against you later.

Then Shirley cried. For once it seemed genuine in a way that her many tearful episodes had never appeared before. Anna reached out and touched Shirley's arm.

'What is the matter. Are you going to be Ok?'

'Please don't tell anyone. Promise me. Now. Please Anna'.

'Of course. It's between you and me but I still don't know what had happened. Tell me'.

'It's that I don't want anyone else to know but we are still seeing each other. Me and Simon.'

'What?' Anna then panicked again. 'Who is this man?'

'He's going to be the new VC.' Shirley did pause for a moment. For effect. But Anna saw Shirley was in genuine distress. For the first time ever in Anna's experience of her.

'What should I do? I don't want my husband to know. But I can't let Simon go. Can I? Not now.'

Anna suddenly realized that her computer was open at the message as she had been going to read it to Joanna. She glanced towards the screen but gratefully saw the screen saver with photos of Dan and the kids flashing to and fro across the screen. Anna thought that she might as well let Shirley talk so she could smile and nod at her. In that way she might gain some important information – but even if she did not - Shirley might feel better.

* * *

CHAPTER 6

THURSDAY

T he next part of the week passed in the usual manner. Students, meetings, some marking, planning grant applications and meeting about ongoing research with current colleagues and associates. It was now Thursday. The day of the first of the formal interviews when there seemed very little doubt that Professor Simon Heath would be seriously considered for the post of Vice Chancellor of the University of South East London. Anna did not know what to do. She could not let herself down by feigning sickness to avoid invovlement. Yet she had no idea how she would handle seeing him again especially after those cryptic messages. She had met with Joanna from HR two days previously but had found it hard to tell her anything and wondered how such a sensitive topic should have landed on such stony, unresponsive ground.

'Hello Professor Brosnan. May I call you Anna?'

'Of course. Joanna! We know each other well. And besides you looked after me during my embarrassing display at the short-listing committee'. Anna was on automatic pilot and was feeling as if she were telling Joanna about a student or colleague. Not about her own deepest fear.

How am I going to broach the subject? I feel a fraud. A fool. But I need to tell her.

'Well you were going to tell me something about the short-listed candidate, I think. Or were you wanting the female candidate to get a chance too? Was that it?'

Joanna was being cheery. She was getting very little information from Anna about why they were meeting and began to wonder whether Anna had contracted flu. Was that the reason for her strange behaviour and the fainting?

'Look. It's difficult and I don't want to waste your time but …. Well many years ago I knew Prof Heath'.

'Oh. Really!' Joanna sounded as though she was being confronted with a confession of a romantic liaison. Staff were now legally obliged to inform HR if they had had a relationship with a student in order to avoid scandal or worse at assessment time. But it was hardly necessary to confess to a relationship among staff – particularly the new VC.

'My God when aren't they in bed together!' Joanna thought. Then: 'No that is unworthy'. Joanna smiled. Anna tried to reciprocate.

I have to do this.

She took a deep breath: 'He raped me'.

'Raped you? When. How?'

Anna almost laughed at this response. When Joanna had looked her in the eye and said that she would log this information Anna almost ran from the room. She looked at her watch, claimed to be late for her class and virtually fled through the door. She was beginning to feel more humiliation by the minute.

Now Anna was in her office trying to psych herself up to attend the interview board.

I need to be calm. I have to look everyone in the eye. Including him. I have to be rational.

Gabriel knocked and came through the door.

'Ready Anna? Come on - let's get this done. It seems as if our choices are limited' he smiled. 'Hey! you look wiped out. What's up?'

'I'm Ok – let's go'.

'I need to go to the office first to collect the interview documents' she squeaked at him. At least that is how it felt as she formed those words. They were being suffocated in her throat which felt as if it her neck was being crushed.

After that they walked together along corridors and down stone steps until they arrived at the Vice-Chancellor's suite where the formal interview was to take place. Anna felt sick. But she also felt as if she were in another world. A dream and it was not her. Nor was she about to come face to face with that man - Simon Heath.

Gabriel and Anna entered the large, formal meeting room. The traditional long, dark, highly polished table was at its heart with ornate, high straight-backed chairs placed on 3 sides. The long side nearest the door had one chair and one filled tumbler of water.

He was going to sit there.

Three water jugs were at the table centre with an empty tumbler, name and status markers and a brown A4 envelope by the chairs. A bureaucratic place setting. No biscuits. No coffee this time. The same people who attended the short-listing gradually made their way into the room. Anna sat down behind the place setting marked Professor A. Brosnan, glancing at the papers she had brought along, affording her some distraction. She caught her breath, nearly knocking over the water jug that the thoughtful man next to her had passed in her direction. Another postcard.

'We have much to catch up with. It won't be long now'.

Anna grabbed the glass of water that her kind neighbour had poured for her. She hoped he hadn't noticed her distress or how violently her hand was shaking.

Ian Fielding, deputy VC arrived, taking his place as the official head of the panel, directly opposite the empty candidate chair next to Joanna from HR. The meeting slowly came to order.

'Following Monday's discussion, it was agreed unanimously to short-list only one candidate. Professor Simon Heath.' And he continued to explain the rules and designate each member of the panel to focus on a specific topic. Anna was to discuss Heath's ideas for encouraging more overseas students in arts and social science subjects. She looked at Joanna.

Was she going to say anything to the panel about Heath? Had she taken note of what I told her? Or was it a dream? Perhaps I never said anything to her.

Joanna clearly wasn't going to say or do anything out of the ordinary and Anna pulled herself up to her full mental height and waited. She had placed the postcard somewhere among the other papers in front of her. She took in another deep breath while Ian Fielding nodded to Joanna to collect the candidate.

Simon Heath, now in his 50s, had retained a full head of straight brown hair which flopped over his forehead in a rather too youthful manner for someone hoping to become a Vice-Chancellor. His eyes were brown, about the same colour as his hair, and his mouth protruded slightly, forced forward by rather large teeth. Anna noticed that although there was an aura of the younger man she had known, a layer of mature heaviness made his neck slightly loose and his collar appear tight. He wore a tweed jacket, brown shirt and yellow tie. This was not the typical senior management veneer. Indeed, Heath looked slightly out of place among colleagues who had, today at least, gone out of their way to appear dark, severe and formal. She realized that most of them would welcome the more relaxed tone that Heath was conjuring up, one that varied markedly from his predecessor. Heath met her eyes, nodded and grinned towards her. Immediately everyone in the room seemed to stare at her and she felt herself turn scarlet with embarrassment, soon turning to anger.

How bloody dare he!

Now she had come face to face with him again Anna felt slightly empowered. He was not the Devil incarnate. In fact he was an averagely attractive looking, overweight, older man. Just the kind she would have liked to see as the VC if she hadn't known his true nature. She already felt she had made a fool of herself but was determined to get through the next two hours.

And then of course tonight we'll have to suffer that bloody dinner arrangement.

It seemed a bit pointless now to have this social event when there was only one candidate, as it was usually taken as a chance to find out what was beneath the surface, but the normal procedure had to be followed and she knew it would not be appropriate to excuse herself.

Then it was her turn to question the candidate. The interview had been bumping along, ticking all the necessary boxes. Most of the panel were looking at their watches or shifting their papers around anxious to get to lunch. She nodded to Fielding, in his role as panel chair, as she addressed her questions to Heath who provided eminently satisfactory answers. After ten minutes Ian Fielding looked at her.

'Do you have any further points to raise Professor Brosnan?'

Anna paused. She was exhausted but then from nowhere that she could fathom came:

'Yes, Professor Fielding. There is one further matter'. She turned towards Simon Heath.

'Professor Heath?'

He nodded with a slightly amused grin.

'What action would you take to deal with a case of sexual violence between a male staff member and a female student?'

There was a change of momentum in the room. Nothing seismic just a mixture of re-engagement and irritation. It was surely time for lunch? And what kind of question is that?

Heath looked at her. It felt as if it were too long.

'Well that is an excellent question. I have talked to my wife and my daughter about some of the dangers of campus life that might go undetected. You find that most people cannot believe that sexual violence – well let's call it rape – could take place in somewhere as civilized as a university. But ...' and he looked at her making her feel uncomfortable ' ... it does, and anyone in authority would need to stamp such behaviour out. Nip it in the bud. Ensure that no-one ever behaves in such a manner. Ever'.

He was so emphatic that Anna sensed in other surroundings there would have been a round of applause. She was dumfounded.

Ian Fielding looked at her questioningly. She nodded to him. And Fielding thanked Simon Heath for his attendance telling him that the panel would now need to discuss his application and looked forward to seeing him for dinner later that day. Joanna scraped back her chair and led Heath from the room. The coffee trolley rattled its way from an ante-room with its wonderful aroma preceding it. Panel members shuffled and looked at each other. Gabriel stood and moved towards Anna, patted her on the shoulder as he went to help Jennie to pass the coffee cups and flasks around the table.

'Great question. Made us all think'. There were some nods and grins. The only person who seemed disturbed apart from Anna was Joanna as she returned to the room. She met Anna's eye as she took her seat.

CHAPTER 7

'Well?' Anna's colleagues Ellie Hart and Donald Delaney were waiting for her in the Psychology Department office.

They had been pressing Sandy, the administrator to contact HR for news and he had tried in vain. So, when Anna and Gabriel returned, they were immediately ambushed.

'Well it seems as if Simon Heath from Littlehampton U is to be confirmed'. Gabriel's assertion drew Shirley and John, their unambitious team mate, into the office to join the others. Shirley was grinning while John made unseemly hand gestures behind her back.

'You look pleased Shirley', Donald ventured. John and Sandy both had to turn away to avoid sniggering.

'Well I am well aware that you all know that Simon and I have a mutual history. And I will thank you to keep your gossip mongering among yourselves.'

Shirley turned to Gabriel.

'I'm told that some woman on the panel implied that sexual assault was common practice in this university. Is that true Gabriel?'

'What that sexual assault is common practice or someone asked?'

'Don't be so defensive please. It's inappropriate. Who asked?'

Anna was watching and listening very carefully to these exchanges.

That woman is so prissy.

Anna moved to intervene.

'Me. What is the problem with that Shirley?'

'Simply that our new VC told me he felt he was being picked on'. She looked at Anna with narrowed eyes.

'I must say I am surprised at you all. Simon is a strong feminist and you have already made him feel that there is hostility to men among the behavioural sciences group. We are not segregationists.'

'Oh? Really? Well ...'

John interrupted at this point. 'Poor little chap eh? It must be hard to feel excluded when you are about to be a VC. Boo Hoo.'

At that point everyone laughed. There followed a mass exodus leaving Sandy, Gabriel's right hand man, to deal with Shirley who was demanding that he give her the regulations on gender equality, harassment and health and safety.

'Shirley! I've told you before. Ask HR.'

Shirley looked down, sniffed loudly and ran from the general departmental office. The others looked at each other and slowly left the room.

Sandy looked around the office making sure it was now empty. He walked to each of the tables scattered around where some of the temporary secretarial staff or occasional postgraduate student would work. He bent down and ran the palm of his hand under each one. Standing between the tables sighing, groaning and stretching his shoulders he then flattened himself against the wall reaching behind the metal filing cabinets and the two big stationery cupboards. Nothing. At least not right now. Like everyone else, with the apparent exception of the new VC, he found Shirley fairly loathsome. He'd made several attempts to tell his boss Gabriel his belief that she had hidden recorders, and possibly even cameras, around the department in order to catch racist remarks or general gossip she might use against whomsoever had upset her.

'She's either a potential blackmailer or she simply wants to be the centre of attention. Either way she is loathsome'.

'Are you talking to yourself or those little men in your head? Anna asked as she returned to the departmental office.

'Ha. Ha. Well actually it was to those little men. Come over here let me show you something.'

Anna went to Sandy's desk looking at him quizzically as he raised his finger to his mouth in a 'shush' gesture. He opened the top drawer of his desk with a key he retrieved from his jeans pocket. He pulled some paperwork aside and pointed. Anna saw a small black object. She touched it and turned it over as far as she was able, given it was stuffed into the mounds of memos and email print-outs. It was a security camera.

'What do ...?'

'Shush' signaled Sandy once again.

The existence of the camera fitted in with the nerdy image the psychologists held of Sandy. He was relatively young – probably around 25 years. Short black hair spiked with a gluey substance and black rimmed glasses. Most of Anna's colleagues found him a joy to have around. He knew where to find things they had misplaced, understood the workings of the organization, knew every other administrator, along with the limits of their authority, and understood the academic system enough to warn anyone who might be stepping into trouble with the competitive back-stabbing elite. No mean feat.

'Anna. I wonder if I might ask you something about the file I put in your office?' and he gestured to her towards the corridor. They moved silently out into the hallway.

'I am convinced that Shirley is using electronic stuff for spying'.

'You're kidding?'

'No not at all. I discovered that camera you saw two weeks ago. Around the time that Hanlon our old VC was predicted to be running out on us. I also found small microphones.

About four of them.'

Anna looked shocked.

'What on earth do you mean?'

'Well ever since I started in this job, she has tried to butter me up. And bloody yuk – it was hard not to vomit'. Anna suppressed a smirk. They were talking about an esteemed colleague and Sandy was only young – she didn't want to give too much away of her own feelings about Shirley. He grinned.

'Don't pretend. I know what you all think of her'.

'Ok. I'll not speak for the others but yes. Ok.'

'So it was behind the stationery cupboard. I found it flashing away just after Gabriel and our lounge lizard friend John had been chatting – well gossiping if you like – but totally harmless ....'

'You mean about Hanlon?'

'Yeh, and who they thought might get the job next of course'.

'And?'

'John said something about Shirley saying she had suggested a good friend of hers to Ian Fielding ....'

'Yes but he's the deputy VC – surely he would be a rival for the post?'

'Come on Anna – you must know that it is unlikely that any university would promote internally at that level?'

Anna noted that Sandy knew more than most about those kind of informal rules and started thinking. It suddenly occurred to her that the past 20 minutes or so had felt *normal*. The usual people taking the usual sides about the goings on around the university.

Just everyday stuff. Maybe I shall survive all this. At least I feel a little easier about the dinner tonight. And as for bloody Shirley Collins – I think I can leave her to Gabriel to manage.

'Ok Sandy. I get what you're telling me. We need to be careful. Nothing more to be done yet though'.

Sandy looked slightly anxious but nodded reluctantly, slammed the drawer and locked it.

BELIEVE ME

* * *

CHAPTER 8

J oanna sat in her office in the HR department.
Gazing out at the elevated railway in the distance she could see the trains line up as some mystery person or computer allocated them to their platform.

She reflected on how much she enjoyed her work at USEL. Previously she had held a junior post at a housing association in north London but after that, she had been a training officer in a less prestigious university. The staff there had seemed to know their place more so than the majority of academics appeared to do. In the housing association, just as at USEL, there had been issues about racism and discrimination which featured most when there were disputes about decision-making. Who was to be allocated the house? Which apartments were suitable for single mothers with young children? And mostly what right did you as a Black woman have to evict a white man for not paying his rent for weeks? Or just as often – vice versa. As a middle-aged white woman married to a Jamaican man, Joanna considered she had an understanding of all sides. But she and her husband, who had a senior position in a local bank, saw the lazy thinking and hypocrisy of most of it.

She was anxious as anyone about the new VC.

Could he deal with the financial situation that Hanlon is leaving us with? Will he replace the ailing HR director who spends too much of his time wining and dining senior management? Will he recognize that the time has come to promote me?

She deliberated too on how to manage the selection din-ner. The original aim was that several short-listed candi-dates would meet the selection panel members informally in advance of the final appointment meeting. But now there seemed to be an acceptance that Prof Heath was the only candidate. He was to be the new VC which meant that the ambience would be different. More of a welcome to meet the senior staff than a test of social skills. It was a bit of a worry. She sighed.

She turned to look out of the window once again. All the trains seemed to move towards their platforms at that mo-ment. Just like pieces of a puzzle falling into place. Until the next tranche. *Anyway, it's not just down to me. But there is that issue of Anna Brosnan. Could that be true? She isn't usually the hysterical type. But on the other hand – I can't imagine anyone being able to force themselves on her. She's far too strong.*

Joanna decided to assume it would be business as usual and arranged for her secretary to proceed as expected. Dinner at 7.30 for 8 at the King William Hotel.

* * *

CHAPTER 9

THURSDAY EVENING

Anna arrived home early.

Dan was in the kitchen bending over a recipe book. His brown hair, already turning grey in places, flopped out of the pony tail. He appeared absorbed in his task as Anna breezed through the door.

'Hi darling. I'm hoping to impress the kids tonight. Beef stroganoff.'

Anna smiled 'I always love your cooking. Can't speak for those brats though'.

'Well Alison has already suggested it's fattening and against modern eco values. But bugger it. If you're out for a posh dinner I'm going to have one too. How about a glass of wine?'

'Yes please! I seriously need something to relax me. I'm kinda dreading ...'

'Do you really need to go? It sounds like a bit of a stitch-up to me anyway. That one guy? Play hooky – why not?'

Anna was sorely tempted. She sipped at the wine Dan poured for her and smiled.

'By the way. A man came to the door earlier. Looking for you. Sorry I almost forgot to tell you'.

'Who?' Anna felt a sudden surge of alarm pass through her body.

'He didn't say. Wouldn't more like. My guess – an old student with a crush'. Dan laughed and stroked Anna's cheek. He was surprised to see she looked shocked. Normally he would expect her to smile and dismiss the whole thing until it arose again.

Anna had no idea why she was worried either.

This is a strange week. Startling. Simon. I guess I expect everything unexpected to scare me. I'm being irrational.

'I'd better go for a shower and get changed. Do you think my black trouser suit would fit the bill? Reasonably expensive hotel restaurant but remembering we are academics? What do you think Dan?'

'Perfect of course. You will look great. Try not to look too great eh? We don't want this new chap taking a shine to you.'

Dan laughed and returned to his recipe book not seeing the shudder passing through Anna. She poured herself another glass of pinot noir – the first had mysteriously vanished – to drink while she was getting ready.

Christ whatever you do don't drink too much! Just enough to relax so no-one knows.

Half an hour later, as she headed for the bottle to top off her glass, the door-bell rang.

'That will be Gabriel with the taxi. Luxury at the university's expense. Means we can drink'. Anna grabbed for her coat.

'Be careful. Not too much. But have fun!' ordered Dan.

Anna opened the door to face a smiling Gabriel in a dark suit and tie. 'Unbelievable! But you look great'.

'You both do' came from Dan as he waved them off in the taxi.

* * *

CHAPTER 10

Driving into London in the evening was a different experience from the early morning commute in the crowded train.

Gabriel and Anna enjoyed themselves, gossiping about colleagues, speculating about promotions and slating one particular professor of economics for a bungled television interview.

'What a buffoon! He thought he sounded so intellectual but really he appeared not to understand his own theories'.

'Nothing as bad as that fool Billy wotsizname – you know the sociologist? Going on about domestic violence on the radio earlier today'.

For some reason they both relaxed into self-righteousness.

'Hey look where we are?'

They both looked out of the car towards the River Thames still shining in the fading early autumn sunshine as they passed through the roundabout south of Lambeth Bridge. Five minutes later they pulled up outside the King William Hotel. Gabriel signed the driver's receipt and Anna gave him a £3 tip. They stepped out and headed towards the incongruous entrance of the grand Victorian building deep in the heart of Waterloo with its railway arches, newspaper sellers and rough sleepers. They were greeted by a liveried doorman, soon after which Joanna appeared from the shadows of the foyer directing them to the cloakroom and conducting them towards the pre-dinner drinks.

'Are you feeling alright?' Joanna asked Anna while Gabriel checked in his coat. Anna didn't understand for a few moments. 'Oh Joanna – yes. Thank you I'm fine'.

Gabriel joined them while Joanna returned to the lobby to look for other arrivals. Gabriel gestured for Anna to go first into the room. She reluctantly did so, thinking that it would look odd to resist. The first person she saw was Simon himself talking to Ian Fielding the deputy VC. It was as if he was programmed to know when she arrived. He met her eyes with a long, dark and amused look. He turned to Fielding, said something quickly and moved in Anna's direction. Simon almost collided with Gabriel who was in the act of handing Anna a large glass of wine. Simon held out his hand.

'Anna how very lovely to see you. Properly this time. No formalities. I have been looking forward to tonight. And you are?' he turned to Gabriel with what Anna thought was guilty haste. They introduced themselves.

'Ah - so you're Anna's boss then?'

The clatter of glasses seemed almost unbearably loud. Anna's nerves were tingling while she attempted to stop her hand holding the wine from shaking.

'I supervised Anna's brilliant doctoral thesis. Did you know?' Gabriel didn't and looked at her quizzically. He hadn't known this but at the back of his mind he had stored her strange reaction to the short-listing meeting.

Was this what it was all about? Did these two have a history?

Gabriel recalled the gossip about Shirley Collins and wondered what on earth was going to happen once this man was in post. It didn't bode well for anyone.

But I don't know this for sure. Maybe she doesn't want to be reminded of her student days.

'Ah Prof Heath please come and meet Sir John Southgate chair of our Council' Joanna led Simon away to the relief of both Anna and Gabriel.

'What is going on Anna?'

'I really don't know. I feel quite upset. A bit disoriented. Can I tell you something Gabriel? In total confidence?'

'Of course. Come on into the lobby we can find a quiet corner'. But just then the head waiter summoned them to dinner and Joanna and her colleagues rounded everyone up herding them into the amazing dining hall. It looked as if it were left over from the Romanov empire. A vaulted ceiling sculpted in blue and gold with white and gold panelled walls. The table, with a bright white heavy linen cloth, silver cutlery, tastefully laden with bowls of fruit and small vases of cut flowers, was at the centre of the room underneath a crystal chandelier.

'How much is this actually costing?' Anna turned to Gabriel in some disgust.

'Don't know but it is odd. It's not a selection process is it? It's like a coronation'.

They were separated at dinner and Anna was placed between two heads of departments – physics, Solly, and IT, Jeff. Like Gabriel they both viewed this occasion with some suspicion. 'Why are we doing this?' Solly asked his dinner companions in a stage whisper which made both Jeff and Anna declare 'Shush!' everyone can hear you. Solly was unrepentant but did keep his voice down after that. It was clear that everyone was perplexed by the apparent failure to find anyone else to compete for the VC post and this exorbitant dinner that had no obvious selection function.

The food they were served rivalled the dinner Dan had been planning at home. More so did the volume and quality of the wine. Anna, against her own advice and intention, was intoxicated. She feared that her mind and body were slightly out of her control. She kept her eyes on Simon all through the meal, but he didn't look in her direction once.

It's almost as if he is blanking me. Trying to get my attention? Bastard.

'I'm going for a pee' she announced to her dinner mates just as the university party was being shepherded from the dining room to the ante-room for liqueurs and coffee. Anna pulled herself away from the group hoping no-one had noticed. She entered the lobby and looked for the sign leading to the washrooms. Slightly woozy she made her way through the muted lighting until she spotted the sign 'Ladies'. She steadied herself and was about to give the door a push when she was grabbed from behind. She stiffened at the same time feeling her pursuer's the warm breath close to her neck, lips brushing her skin and a man holding her to his body. A wave of anger swept through her as the hands holding her tightened around her waist. She struggled to face her assailant. No surprise.

'What do you want? Please let go of me.'

'We are going to be working together soon. I'm excited about that. Aren't you?'

Anna wanted to punch him.

'Let go please Simon. I really need to pee'.

'I'll wait here. Don't be long I'm dying to talk to you'.

She pushed the washroom door open. No-one else was there and she went into a cubicle shaking, experiencing a sense of unreality. She had little awareness of time passing until there was a loud knocking on the cloakroom door and Simon put his head through.

'Anna! Where are you? Is everything alright?'

'I'm Ok Simon. Won't be long'.

Krikes. He's controlling me and I'm falling for it.

She couldn't work out what to do next.

He is to be my boss. The VC. Why doesn't anyone else know what he's like? Can't they see? I need to tell Gabriel. Joanna too. They need to believe me. But then what?

She felt completely sober now, washed her hands, dabbed water on her face, left the cloakroom and moved across the lobby towards the room where coffee was being served.

'Ah there she is.' It was Ian Fielding the well-liked deputy VC. 'Prof Heath has been asking for you. Have you seen him? You didn't tell me he had been your PhD supervisor?'

'I didn't want to show bias', Anna muttered in a thin, whiny voice far removed from her normal one. She felt weak, very tired and utterly defeated. She could not work out why.

I guess you can never defeat the system but he knows how to manage it.

Even though she knew that she had not taken up any kind of challenge, so was in no position to win or to lose, she still had the feeling she had lost some kind of contest.

✳ ✳ ✳

CHAPTER 11

Anna was sleepy as she and Gabriel climbed into the waiting taxi.

As soon as it had seemed reasonable Gabriel wanted to go home: 'Are you Ok to leave soon?'

'Most definitely. Now would be good.' And so they collected their coats telling the hotel reception to call their taxi.

'Better say good night to Fielding though' suggested Gabriel. They both pressed their way through the assembled gathering. Anna kept her eyes on Gabriel's retreating shoulders trying not to notice who was on either side of them. As Gabriel reached Ian Fielding, Anna was just behind him. Then she felt her sleeve tightening. Someone was pulling at her jacket hard enough to wrench her off course.

Him.

'Well I'll be seeing you again tomorrow eh?' she looked startled. 'At the formal interview of course'.

Hell. I forgot this nightmare is still running. I've got to be on the selection panel again tomorrow.

Anna nodded. She even managed a smile for Simon as she reached over to touch Ian Fielding's arm in a gesture of polite, friendly appreciation for the evening. Fielding, a hard-working, straightforward man with an academic background in chemistry had always been a favourite among his colleagues. 'You know what you're getting with Ian' was the unanimous verdict. Several influential colleagues would have chosen

Fielding for the VC post despite the unwritten rule that an outsider was needed for the top job. The tenet made some kind of sense – no internal baggage. But within disciplines, as Anna knew only too well, toxic baggage was far from uncommon. She had had no idea until earlier in the week that Simon and Donald Delaney had any connection.

What was that about? And bloody Shirley too?

She was a little worried that Donald, one of her favourite colleagues, was so enthusiastic about Simon's arrival.

Donald must never find out what happened to me. But he needs to know what Simon is really like. And then Sandy – the surveillance. Surely Shirley wasn't doing that? Sandy has to be mistaken. But if not Shirley – who?

And then, like so many of the thoughts Anna had had that week she told herself that she had no idea what to do next.

Gabriel was clearly tired and neither of them had half of the energy and enthusiasm that had characterized their journey on the way to the dinner. Gabriel who had been slumping on the back seat of the taxi sat up, stretched his arms and rubbed his eyes. Anna was expecting him to turn around and rest his head against the window. Instead he said:

'I don't really know what's going on with the VC appointment, do you? It really makes no sense'.

Anna's mind jerked to attention although it wasn't easy through the fog of wine, food and general weariness.

'I mean there's nothing particularly outstanding about him. Good that he is a social scientist. Ok that he was senior at the University of Littlehampton. But ....'

'Are you about to say something patronizing?' Anna laughed in spite of herself.

'Probably' Gabriel smiled. 'But come on you know what I mean. There were other good CVs among the applications – including at least one woman. How on earth did we make the decision to narrow the field down to one man? And this one. Why?'

Anna wanted to know the answer to that question too.

'Oh Anna – I forgot - what were you going to tell me?'
She froze and tried to look vague.
'When?'
'You know. You had something confidential just before the dinner'.
'Um. Yeh. True. It'll keep. We're nearly at my place now Gabriel. It could have been a worse evening though couldn't it?'
Gabriel smiled 'I'll pay the tip this time! See you in the morning'.
The taxi pulled up outside Anna's home and she climbed out managing to remember her bag and jacket which made her feel slightly in control and a little more confident that she could cope with the near future.

❋ ❋ ❋

CHAPTER 12

FRIDAY

Anna was behind her desk early the following morning. She had had to postpone several tutorials because of the VC selection while her unread email list was growing exponentially. She said goodbye to Kim, the second student of the morning, and turned towards the computer.

The pinging of new arrivals to the email list drew her attention.

I don't know where to start.

She looked at her watch. She had about 40 minutes before she had to leave her office. At least there were no more CVs to examine. The panel were each to ask a few clarifying questions to Simon Heath and then introduce themselves and their work to him in expectation of his accepting the VC post.

As if! Huh.

She couldn't decide whether to check down through her list to look at the oldest unread emails or start with the new ones. As she realized she was staring at the screen mindlessly, weighing up the pros and cons of this ridiculous conundrum, there was a knock on her door which opened to a rather stressed looking Donald Delaney. He wasn't holding the customary entreating coffee cup, but neither had she made any yet. Both things surprised her.

'Donald! I'm so pleased to see you. It seems like ages since we've had a chance to catch up. How are you?'

'Well my daughter is still experiencing pain in her arms. My wife is moaning as much as ever. My son wants to become a plumber rather than do A levels. And how about you?'

'I'm tired'.

'After the dinner last night?'

'Well' hesitating. 'Yes partly. But to be honest I am not sure that Simon Heath is the best person for the VC post – but if he accepts it – it's his. What do you think?'

'I've told you. I think he's a good bloke'.

That was a brusque reply. What's got in to Donald?

Anna had been going to tell Donald something about what was behind her reservations but something made her feel uneasy. She had never felt like this in his company before and couldn't explain it.

I need to go with my hunch here. Something is wrong.

'So what else then Donald?'

'Oh nothing out of the ordinary. I wanted to know how the dinner went that's all'.

'Nothing to report. I had some nice chats with colleagues I don't normally see but … well nothing'.

Donald looked at her and all of a sudden Anna decided that this man was no longer that trusted friend. It was a horrible sensation and all the shared confidences, jokes, alliances and mutual support occasions skimmed through the back of her mind as she watched him. He didn't meet her eye. And strangely they sat in silence. Almost for too long as it felt as if there was nothing more to say to each other. Forever, maybe.

How very odd. But this is the end of something. It's so sad.

'Ok. I need to go to the selection meeting now. I'll report back as and when.' And she stood up giving him little option than to do the same. Something was broken and she believed it had to be connected to Simon. How? She didn't know and couldn't imagine. But this unconscious pain, probably for both of them, felt as if it were leaving her with an acute emptiness. A fluttering memory of what had happened all those years ago.

* * *

CHAPTER 13

Gabriel caught up with Anna as she passed the departmental office door giving a wave to Sandy.

Gabriel looked relaxed enough she thought. So did Sandy.

'Hey Anna! I've got a message for you' Sandy left his desk to chase Anna and Gabriel along the corridor.

'Oh? I'm not expecting anything. Is it urgent?'

'Well the guy seemed pretty desperate actually. Anyway, I told him what you were doing this morning and that you couldn't be disturbed. He'd like to see you at 4pm. Is that Ok? Can I tell him?'

By that time Anna and Gabriel were walking fast and Anna told Sandy that that would be alright.

'I should be back by then. See you later'.

I have been neglecting my tutees lately. And it's the start of term too. I need to get this bloody stuff out of the way and return to what is really important. It'll keep me sane.

She swept it out of her mind. They crossed the quadrangle to the VCs suite. There was a chill in the air. The beginning of autumn or some internal chill. She couldn't decide. They turned left along the short corridor with the VC's staff offices, Ian Fielding's room and the large formal interview room. Anna and Gabriel were both pleased to note the sound of coffee cups with the promise of biscuits resonating from the ante-room from which Jennie emerged with the ubiquitous trolley. Jennie made a 'shoo shoo' motion chasing them towards their seats where she served them their coffee, a glass of water and a plate of chocolate chip cookies baked in the university kitchens that morning.

Anna grinned down the table to where Gabriel sat with a cookie braced to enter her mouth. She bit into it and sat back in her chair, relaxing as she nodded to colleagues most of whom were doing the same thing. Then as she glanced over her coffee cup she realized her designated place was directly opposite the empty chair where Simon would be sitting with Ian Fielding and the chair of Council Sir John Southgate's place tags one each side of her.

Why I am in this position?

Anna looked around for Joanna who in her HR capacity was in charge of such things. But too late Sir John and Ian took their seats and Ian opened the proceedings. The assembled selection panel were reminded of their unanimous decision to short list the one candidate who was to be there this morning.

'Professor Simon Heath, currently at Littlehampton University'.

As if we didn't know.

There were some wry grins and nods around the room. Anna noted Ian and Sir John, in contrast, as being stony faced.

Well I suppose they are in charge but this whole business has seemed unusual.

'Please take your seats all of you' Sir John looked grave.

How odd. What's going on now.

'We had intended to offer the post of VC to Professor Heath this morning, to consider his ideas on university development going forward ....'

I hate that phrase.

'But' Sir John continued 'in the light of some very recent developments we are forced to postpone this appointment'.

There was a loud gasp from the assembled panel, including from Anna. She caught Gabriel's eye and both raised their eyebrows. Anna then felt a sense of terror. She looked over at Joanna. She could see Joanna had been watching her because immediately she looked away and then down at the papers on her desk. Joanna was blushing. Others were muttering to each other and then all eyes were on Sir John.

Oh God. What has Joanna said? I didn't give her permission. Nuts. This is nothing to do with me. I'm being paranoid.

Sir John cleared his throat. 'There has been a very serious allegation. Brought by a member of this panel toward Professor Heath when he was a junior lecturer at the London School for Social and Psychological Sciences. There is to be an internal investigation before we are able to take the appointment further. And, in the meantime, Professor Fielding will be acting VC. This as from today'.

Smiles and nods broke out around the table. Fielding had always been popular among the professorial and head of department groups because he was seen to be straightforward and fair.

'And for your information the Metropolitan Police are involved and will no doubt be wanting to interview some or all of you in the next few days'.

Total silence. Some mouths hung open. People looked at each other. Heads shook.

Martin Gittings, one of the few Black British professors at USEL, spoke asking what everyone else wanted to know.

'May we ask the nature of the allegation? How it has only just come to light? I think it is important that we are told'.

'I'm sorry no. But you will find this out soon enough from the police officers. Now I am afraid we need to end this meeting. Joanna will be getting in touch to let you know when we are to reconvene. All being well that will be soon'.

And with that Sir John and Ian stood, scraped back their chairs and marched from the room. Loud chatter burst forth and someone asked Jennie for more biscuits. Anna looked around and stood to move towards Gabriel. But before she could step very far Joanna was by her side, grabbing her arm and steering her into the ante-room with its wonderful smell of coffee and recently baked biscuits.

'What's this Joanna? Is it about what I told you?'

'Yes. But. Well not just you it seems. A man has approached us. He has told me something I cannot share with anyone right now.'

'What? You're kidding. What's happened?' Anna had a feeling she had been here before. Something was rotten. Something she didn't understand was happening and it connected her to Simon Heath in a way that disgusted her.

❁ ❁ ❁

CHAPTER 14

FRIDAY

Anna, alarmed by the events at the aborted appointment panel, returned to her office and sat facing her computer unable to open her email account.

She couldn't explain it, even to herself, but everything about her office suddenly felt toxic.

It's like poison is going to come at me whatever I do. Why has any of this happened?

She put her elbows on her desk, laid her face on her upturned hands and began to sob uncontrollably.

This is not me. I don't recognize this person in my body any more. Hell! that sounds psychotic.

She decided she needed to go home. It was the end of the first week of the autumn term. It was usually an exciting time in the academic calendar. Students making progress. New students arriving with their enthusiasms. Research grants waiting. Papers published and plans for further achievements. And often, most of all, seeing old colleagues after the long summer recess. But that had been spoilt.

What has happened with Donald? I used to trust him above all others. Even above Gabriel. But now? There's something I can't understand.

She took a tissue from her case and wiped her eyes blotting the smudge marks from her eyeliner. She looked at herself in the small mirror she had propped up by the computer screen and headed for the departmental office to speak with Sandy. He was at his desk staring at his computer screen. He looked up as she entered.

'What is the matter Anna? You look in a bad way.'

She attempted to dismiss his remark with characteristic humour but failed.

'I don't feel great actually. I am going home. Can you let everyone know please? I'll just call in and tell Gabriel. I'm sure I'll be ready for Monday. This has been an odd week.'

'Only thing Anna – a woman from the Met Police was looking to speak with you. Literally five minutes ago. I was just coming to warn you. I have her mobile. She wanted you to call her. And that bloke – from earlier?'.

'Shit. Please tell the student – I'm guessing – to make another appointment. But what about the bloody police?'

As Sandy handed over a memo with Inspector Dorothy Whitaker's mobile number she felt her hands shake. Sandy looked enquiringly but had enough tact not to say anything.

'I'll go to see Gabriel and then call her from home. Thanks again Sandy – have a good weekend. Next week will be better I'm certain of that.'

She managed a grin and a wave and headed for Gabriel's office. She knocked, opened the door and was about to step in when Gabriel looked up shook his head at her. With his back to the door and facing Gabriel's desk was Donald Delaney. Anna nodded at Gabriel, returned to her office to collect her things and headed out from the main campus for the 20-minute walk to Waterloo station.

* * *

CHAPTER 15

She puzzled again about what was going on with Donald. And what was going on with Simon and the university. And what did DI Dorothy Whitaker want with her? The journey home seemed endless. Anna was grateful to have a seat on the train, but she couldn't face reading a novel or the Evening Standard which she usually did when Gabriel wasn't with her. It took so long to reach each station and the wait at the platforms was endless. But at last the announcement 'We are now approaching Endlesham Station' reached her ears. She hauled herself and her case up from the seat and headed for the carriage door. The fresh air as she stepped from the carriage lightened her mood slightly.

As much as I love London it is always great to get home away from the claustrophobic atmosphere.

As usual only a few people got out at her station. She knew Dan would be home thinking about their evening meal and how they might spend the coming weekend.

I'm going to have to explain the police interview to him. And should I say anything about Simon?

She never had done. There had been no need. She had never seen Simon again after 'that' had happened. And it hadn't impacted on her family life with Dan or their love for each other. In fact, she had kept the memory of Simon very much out of conscious reach until this week. Now it felt as though everything with him had happened only yesterday and what he had done had always been part of who she had become.

Anna decided to walk home from the station. She often did so but Dan also liked to meet her and drive her home.

'You've been working and you're carrying all this stuff. Go out for a walk later if you want.'

Unusually Anna chose to take a slightly longer route home. Through the park and up the hill rather than along the main road.

Thinking time.

She needed to prepare how she was going to break things to Dan. Also she didn't want to face questions from the police inspector before she had run everything through her own mind even though she had no real certainty about what DI Whitaker wanted to discuss. Most of all Anna hadn't yet gained any sense of relief that Simon might not actually become the new VC. Only last night she had hoped that he would decide not to take the job. But now she felt far too uncomfortable to take pleasure that he might not be the boss after all.

How did it all become so dramatic? And now of all times? But why do I feel so anxious still?

It was still early in the afternoon and the sun was out. It was bright and warm but the day didn't reflect her current mood. It did however allow her to ease the tension in her shoulders and back and slowly recall that time, almost 20 years ago, before her real life had begun.

We were more like school girls than postgrads!

Simon had been their tutor. They were a group of 5 – 4 women, Anna, Tina, Michelle and Nancy, and a man. Strangely she couldn't recall anything about him except his name. Michael.

I think he had dark hair. I think he was clever. Why can't I remember?

Nancy was gay. She thought men were ungainly, clumsy and often unpleasantly smelly. She would tease the other 3 and was scornful about their collective crush on Simon.

'You are thinking of him as a super-stud professor who will carry you to the top of university life! But really he is a creepy guy with an eye for the main chance. He'd sleep with any and each of you if he could manage it seamlessly. He has a wife and child you know?'

That was the first time Anna had seen him as a person with a life rather than the object of her passion. She was strangely shocked. Brought to her senses about him. She wondered how his wife managed to live with him. He was always in his office or the student union bar in the evenings. Even the postgrad students had work that limited their evening leisure. But not Simon apparently. He would typically be leaning on the corner of the bar, pint in hand, and shamelessly looking the female students up and down. He was rarely alone with his pint for long. Young women would flock round him, standing very close, fluttering their eyes and moving their bodies. There was an atmosphere of sensuality about these encounters with Simon that differed from other mixed gender groups. Anna knew because she and her friends would try to be the ones flirting with him.

Such a long time ago.

Not for the first time this week Anna attempted to recall how she and Simon had ended up alone in her flat drinking. On that toxic night. It had been Michelle's birthday and she had wanted a gin and tonic celebration. So they embarked on a gin-filled evening beginning with a bottle shared between them in Michelle's room before moving to a fashionable bar just south of the river where they consumed several more. Michael had been with them too.

That was odd. He was with us but I can't recollect anything he said or did. But he was there.

Anna sighed. She returned her mind to the present as she crossed the field along the river bank known as Endlesham Flats. She could now see ahead to where the land rose steeply through the wooded track that led to Endlesham Heights where she lived. She had lost track of the time but realized she was walking slowly. She noticed that the sun was fading when suddenly her mobile phone shuddered in her handbag.

'Hi darling.'

'Where are you? I've just called Sandy who told me you had left a couple of hours ago. He said you felt unwell'.

'Yes a little. I'm coming up through the woods now. I'll be home in 15. And ....'

'What?'

'Well there is something I need to discuss with you'.

It was unnerving being back in the real world. Anna's reminiscences had brought to mind the missing years. That young woman had gone now. If only that night hadn't happened. If only Simon had not been at that bar.

* * *

CHAPTER 16

Anna had rarely been so pleased to get home.

Dan opened the front door ready to greet her with his characteristic smile. As she crossed the threshold, kissing him, she could hear the whirring and squeaking from twins' electronic game.

'God that is awful. Should we let them?'

'They've done their homework' Dan shrugged 'at least I think so'.

At that point Alison emerged from the kitchen clutching a glass of soya milk.

'Hello darling'. Anna went to kiss her but received a dark look.

'Why do *they* get everything they want? I have to do my homework upstairs. I can't stand this place any more'.

Dan and Anna exchanged looks trying to suppress smiles as Alison stormed past them.

'Hey ho. Do you think the boys will be like this in a couple of years?' They laughed together.

'But what do you want to tell me? It sounded important. And you're unwell. What's going on? Here – put your bags down and I'll get some tea and we can talk.'

'Thank you' she smiled.

Anna perched on the edge of an armchair holding out her cupped hands for the mug of tea that Dan brought her. He sat on another armchair facing her looking down at his tea.

He's trying to make it easy for me. Being casual. But I know he is really worried. I have to tell him.

'Dan there's no easy way to say this ....'

He jerked backwards spilling a little of his tea.

God I think he thinks I want to leave him.

'No. No. Nothing like that' she said.

'It's from a very long time ago. Something I didn't tell you. There was no need really. It was in the distant past. But – well. I'll tell you'.

Dan nodded. Looked at her. She gained some strength. It was as if he had felt it was the worst but now knew it wasn't.

'When I was a graduate student my supervisor raped me'.

Anna felt calm. She was talking about someone else. Someone she didn't know. Dan gasped. She held her hand up towards him in an attempt to soothe him.

'It was awful. Awful. But I always thought it was partly my fault ... '

'Nonsense! Whoever it was knew what he was doing. The bastard'.

Suddenly tears sprung from her eyes. This had become real. About her now. Dan moved over towards her, taking her mug from her, placing it on the coffee table and holding her. She broke into sobs. Anna noticed that her neck was damp.

Dan is crying too!

And that made her cry even more.

'Mum. Dad.' The door had burst open and Alison was standing there. 'What's going on? And when's dinner?'

'Give us a few moments darling' Dan managed. She retreated from the room but quietly. Fleetingly Dan realized that Alison could be kind and thoughtful too. Sometimes. He returned to his chair, giving Anna back her mug of tea and she drank a few mouthfuls gratefully.

'But why are you so upset now? Has he tried it again?'

'No' Anna laughed between tears. 'No. But you know who was to be appointed as our new VC?'

'Not him?'

'Yes! Simon Heath. It was him. I heard things about over the years – the usual. As you do with colleagues in similar areas. Promotions. Research grants. You know?'

'When does he start?'

'Well that's just it. I made an idiot of myself at the short-listing – fainted'

'What?'

'Yeh. Totally stupid. But I told Joanna – a senior HR person. She didn't seem to pay much attention. So. Well I saw him. At that bloody dinner.'

'No? how terrible – did you speak to him'

'Well he tried to speak to me. But what is important is that the next day, when we thought he would be crowned – there was no competition. He was the only candidate. Well we were told this morning at that meeting that there were 'issues'. We couldn't confirm his appointment and Ian would be interim VC'.

'Well that's good isn't it?'

'But I don't know why. Joanna didn't tell me she was going to say anything. And, well – maybe someone else came forward. I really don't know. But the police – a female inspector – Whitaker – yes that's her name wants me to phone her. Now. Today.'

'Ok. Drink your tea. Rest for a bit and phone her. See what's going on. What she wants.' Dan then leant over and kissed her. She looked away from him down towards her hands. She realized she was fiddling with her wedding ring. Twisting it around.

'I always had a feeling that there was something. Only it took so long for you to tell me.'

✱ ✱ ✱

CHAPTER 17

Anna sat at the desk in her study with pen and paper ready as she dialed DI Whitaker's number. The inspector came straight to the point.

'There have been serious allegations made about Simon Heath. I understand that you yourself have informed your HR department?

'Yes. Yes I did but …'

'You will know of course that rape is a serious crime?'

'Of course. But …'

'Professor Brosnan I am 5 minutes away from your home now. I am coming to speak to you about the allegations. I shall see you then'.

And as DI Whitaker hung up Anna stared at the phone and Dan knocked softly at the open door of her study.

'There's a car just pulled into the drive. I am guessing that is your police officer?'

'It must be'. Anna felt flat, detached, without any desire to bring up her past again. Dan knew now, and that was all that mattered to her. Dan opened the door before DI Whitaker had the chance to knock, introduced himself before ushering her into the living room.

'I know you're here to see Anna. She'll be with you in a moment. Would you like some tea?'

'No thank you.' She turned at the sound of footsteps and stood. 'Ah Professor Brosnan. I am Inspector Whitaker. Dorothy.'

She smiled at Anna who was looking pale. Anna, who had been trying to make herself alert had brushed her hair and splashed cold water on her face and neck. She entered the room running a hand over her damp face and held out her hand 'It's Anna. Thank you for coming so quickly'.

'Ah. I have just been visiting a colleague of yours. Professor Gabriel Watson'.

'Of course he is just along the road. Please sit down'.

Dorothy Whitaker was younger than Anna had expected. She was probably around 30. Her bright blond hair was neatly cut. She wore a dark brown tight skirt along with a blue silk blouse which made her look human and relaxed. That she had kicked off her black spiked heeled shoes as she greeted Anna, enhanced that image although Anna wondered why she wore such things in the first place.

'Ok. I think you already have a good idea of what I need. It's about Simon Heath. I understand from your HR department that you claim he raped you? Around 20 years ago I understand.'

'Yes'. Anna hesitated. She was feeling upset but more so really angry.

'Why were you told this? I had no intention of calling the police. I was upset when I understood that Heath was to be our new Vice Chancellor. It was really stupid. I fainted. I told our HR person what had happened. And I was going to meet with her properly – to let her know the details. But that meeting never happened. And then at the last minute we were told formally that Simon Heath's appointment was to be held up. We were told there were 'issues'.'

'Yes. I'm afraid there are and they're based on your allegations'.

Anna looked shocked and was aware of Dan hovering near the door. He was looking out for her as usual.

'Dan please come and sit with us. Is that Ok – er Dorothy?'

'If you are comfortable with that of course'.

'I've told my husband what happened. But only today. It was so awful at the time. I put it all behind me. I wanted to forget it. And mostly I have. Until this week when it seemed he was to be our new VC.' Anna began shaking. Dan lent over and grabbed her hand.

'I still don't understand who told the police. I didn't want to make a fuss. If I had, I guess I'd have said something at the time'.

'Ah yes. This was to be one of the starting points. What did you do at the time?'

'It was awful' she sobbed, wiped her eyes and pulled herself together. 'It was at my flat. My friend's birthday celebration – I was drunk. We all were. Simon was at the bar and before I knew it he was with us as we walked home and he ended up in my apartment. We had another bottle of wine. I think I must have passed out because I only remember being hurt. Terrible pain. Him on top of me.' She shivered. Dan squeezed her hand once again. She realized this must be upsetting him. Maybe even more than she was disturbed having to relive the experience. She turned to him.

'I'm so sorry!'

'It was not your fault. Please don't say that'.

But Anna had always felt it had been. She had lost control. She had blocked out much of what happened. She had no recollection, even now, as to how she ended up with Simon at her apartment.

'Before he left – Oh God – it was awful. He kissed me and I felt so ..... so well cheap. So tawdry'. She pulled away from Dan and put her head in her hands covering her eyes and letting her dark red hair fall forward like a blanket obscuring the scene playing out in her own home.

This is not happening. I hate myself.

'I was not quite 21 when this happened. Just started my PhD. I was supposed to be some kind of whizz kid at the time. I had a scholarship. I had only ever had sex with one boyfriend when I was an undergraduate. We had broken up and I was mostly studying. Anything else was having fun with my girlfriends. Michelle, Tina and Nancy. Nancy is gay so we didn't really spend much time looking for men. Not really.'

'Ok take your time. You're doing fine'. Anna had started shaking again. Her mouth was dry and each word grated on her throat. She caught sight of Dan from the corner of her eye. He was pale. In shock probably.

I so wish he didn't have to hear this. Does he think it was my fault now?

'What more can I tell you?'

'Did you tell your girlfriends?'

'No' Anna hesitated. 'It was because Michelle and Tina fancied him. So did I. That was the problem. That's why I think it has to be my fault'. Her voice was loud and shrill now. Dan stroked her arm which made her feel a great deal better. She had worried he would despise her.

'You're being very brave' he whispered. 'Please tell Dorothy everything. This man deserves to go down'.

Dorothy gave him a stern look but he ignored it.

'Please go on Anna. What did you do after …. Afterwards?'

'I cried. I was still drunk. I stayed lying on the floor and cried. Then I must have fallen asleep because it was about 4 a.m. when I got up and stood in the shower for about an hour. Put a wash on with all the clothes I was wearing.' She hesitated. 'And then I cried. And then I had some more wine. After that I don't recall but I never went back to my tutorial group.'

'Didn't your friends want to know what was wrong?'

'I wrote to them. Said I was ill and went home to my parents. I carried on with my thesis. I got a job in a book store. And then changed to a different university to finish the PhD. I didn't hear from anyone after a few weeks. Since then I've bumped into them at conferences and all seems fine. None of us ever asks about the time I disappeared. And overall it was only a very short time from my life. They've probably forgotten. And to a point so had I until ….'

Anna then wept. Uncontrollably this time. Dan moved over

to hold her and Dorothy whispered.

'Any chance we might all have that tea now?'

'Of course' and he slowly released himself from Anna and moved to the kitchen. Dorothy touched her arm.

'Let's wait for a little. You need to recover. It is clear that this has all been a shock. But you are recalling things now that are essential for us to see whether there is a case to be answered.'

Anna nodded and ran her hand across her face, looked up at Dorothy and tried to smile. Dan arrived with the tea. Then a sudden noise resembling an avalanche surprised them all as the twins and Alison came down the stairs yelling at each other and demanding their dinner. This brought Anna back to the present.

'I'll sort all this out and get dinner underway.' Dan offered. 'Would you like to move into Anna's study?' He headed for the kitchen and the children. Anna led Dorothy into her study.

'There's not a great deal more to tell you'.

'That is fine. You've been very helpful. For now. But I shall be back in touch after I have taken our inquiries further'.

Anna saw her visitor out. She wasn't sure she could face the full force of the family just at that time and retreated into her study closing the door. She brought her computer out of sleep and began to scan her emails. And then she started. Gasping, she held her hand over her mouth.

Oh God! I remember now. There was someone else there. Behind the door.

She began shaking again and the whole scene returned to her mind. The pain. The humiliation. The absolute *fear*. She didn't know what to do. She couldn't face the family right now. She had to compose herself. She then opened her emails out of habit and scanned down the long list of unopened ones. Then she spotted an email from **Simon@Little.ac.uk**

✳ ✳ ✳

CHAPTER 18

MONDAY

Anna had little memory of Friday evening - how she had got through the family dinner, helped Alison with some of her homework and cleared away the dishes after the meal.

The weekend itself had disappeared from her memory too. She remembered avoiding a neighbour's drinks party and felt she was being unfair to Dan. He had been amazing since she had told him what had happened. Or told him some of it. She hoped she would be as supportive and loyal if their situations were ever to be reversed. But she was certain too that he would have questions, and right now she did not want to answer anything.

'Thank you.' Anna and Dan lay in bed. She gripped his hand and he put his arms around her.

'Take your time. You can tell me everything when you're quite ready'.

This is why I married him. I must hold on to him.

Incredibly they both slept until the alarm woke them at 7. Then it was chase the children. Feed the children. Shower. Dress. *Jeans and black blouse.* Eat. *Muesli with honey and Alpro.* Pack. *Student assignments and notes for research grant meeting.* Set out for the station. *Catch the 8.15 for Waterloo.*

I hope Gabriel has kept a seat free me more. I don't think I can manage to stand for 40 minutes.

Fellow travellers had taken up their usual positions on the

platform at Endlesham Station. Several were on nodding terms. Anna was no exception and it gave her courage to see that this world was the same as it always had been. As the train drew in, she saw Gabriel's black jacket and balding head near the front of their usual carriage.

But he's not looking for me.

Anna stepped into the carriage which was not full yet and headed in his direction until she realized – he had not kept a seat for her. There were a few available but not near to Gabriel. In a trance she settled between a man who insisted on keeping his large thighs parted and a young woman with headphones who was eating a bacon sandwich.

Ugh. This is unbearable.

Even so she decided to stay there. She felt a pain in her chest like someone had hit her with a hammer.

Gabriel. He's ignoring me. No - it's worse. What is going on?

She saw that Gabriel was talking to the man next to him.

Oh, perhaps he's with a friend. That might explain it.

As they reached Clapham Junction the man stood up and left the train. It was the man she had seen before at this station. The one who had given her a friendly smile.

Was that only last week? What will Gabriel do when we get to Waterloo?

Anna's questions were answered as the train pulled in to the platform accompanied by apologetic announcements over the speaker system telling the weary commuters that they were waiting for an available platform. Anna paused while the man with the thighs and the woman, who had now fin-ished her sandwich, stood up and moved along the central aisle of the carriage. She waited as Gabriel approached. He saw her and nodded.

No smile.

'Hi Anna. I'll catch up with you later. I've got to go some-where before work. See you in the department'.

That was the first time he had ever failed to walk with her. The week was not off to a good start. Anna felt despondent as she walked along the platform, past the ticket barrier, down the steps leading from the station. The day was bright but feeling colder than expected as she emerged. The black taxis streamed down the hill from their rank tooting impatiently at the barrage of passengers escaping from their trains into their daily routines. Anna headed towards the main road following the clusters of students who gained momentum as more materialized from buses and side roads to join their ranks. Despite everything, Anna always enjoyed being surrounded by these young people whose lives were bustling with excitement. Even so, she wondered how many would still be as energized and happy in 10 years' time as they seemed to be today.

This human torrent, with Anna in their midst, arrived at the campus where everyone dispersed towards their particular lectures and departments. The stairs and corridors leading to the Psychology Department seemed deserted. She went straight to Sandy's domain to collect mail and any messages. He looked up at her, raising his eyebrows, almost as a warning and pointed his head towards a desk at the far end of the office near the stationery cupboard. There, Donald Delaney was sitting with his arm around the shoulder of Shirley Collins - his erstwhile nemesis, or so everyone had been led to believe. She had tears streaming down her face.

Try something new for Heaven's sake! It's always tears with you.
Through her wet, swollen eyes she stared at Anna.

'How could you? You've just ruined his life. He's a good man. You are a bloody cow!'

Sandy, Donald and Anna all jerked to attention at that outcry. 'Ok. Ok. Anna it's better if you leave the office for now' said Donald. And Anna in complete shock and amazement complied. She went to her own office stunned. She put her case down on the floor next to her desk. Sat at her desk chair. Rubbed her eyes staring at the blank screen. She turned the computer on, waiting for it to boot up. There was a soft knock at the door and Sandy entered. He closed the door behind him and sat down next to her in the chair usually occupied by students.

'Sorry about that. I really am. That woman has been sitting in my office looking for anyone who will hear her story. Then Donald came along. And I cannot imagine how it happened. But he started being nice to her'.

Sandy pulled a face and Anna laughed. He was a great person to have on her side right now.

'But Donald hates her.'

'So does everyone else. I have no idea what on earth he is thinking about. But, Anna look' and he delved into the pocket of his jeans producing a memory stick.

'Don't tell anyone please. It's more than my job's worth. But I've taken a copy from one of the recorders she stashed behind the filing cabinet. You know I showed you?'

Anna nodded.

'Well as you know they were not there the other day. But they're back now. I'm not going to warn Donald because I think he's playing a game'.

'What do you mean?'

'Well he began to attack me towards the end of last week. Told Gabriel that I wasn't keeping the student records up to date'.

'What? Everyone knows you're the best thing ......'

'Thanks Anna. And Gabriel backed me up. But Donald. The ever-lovable Donald seems to have changed. So please be careful yourself. I've got to go.'

He left and Anna was even more perplexed. There was still something she had to do and do now. She'd avoided it last night. And with that she opened the email from Simon. It was dated Sunday night at 10.37 p.m.

HOW COULD YOU DO THIS TO ME? YOU KNOW IT ISN'T TRUE. I THOUGHT MORE OF YOU THAN THIS. I PLAN TO CONTEST YOUR ACCUSATIONS SO BE WARNED. YOU WON'T COME OUT OF THIS SO WELL YOURSELF. I HAD HOPED WE MIGHT CONTINUE WHERE WE HAD LEFT OFF ALL THOSE YEARS AGO.
REGARDS SIMON

What does he mean? I won't come out of this well? Out of what?
Anna realized that she had spent more time sobbing over the last few days than ever before in her life.
Except for then.
And then she noticed that Sandy had left the memory stick on her desk.

❉ ❉ ❉

CHAPTER 19

Anna placed the memory stick in her case.
It's better to wait till I get home.
She tried to make sense of how her morning had gone so far.

Well – my friend and boss Gabriel avoided me. Donald has changed sides. Simon is threatening me, and Sandy has given me a weapon. But who am I supposed to be fighting? How did any of this begin?

It was almost 10 a.m. and she was expecting a stream of individual tutorials any minute that would last until lunch time. She gathered her thoughts and her emotions ready to deal with the psychology of bystander apathy.

By 1 p.m. her self-belief had been restored. It was her students who made her feel positive. Useful.

But I shouldn't have to rely on other people to make me feel good. I've done nothing wrong.

But it was difficult to convince herself of that. Her sense of goodness was taken from her 20 years ago and try as she had, she couldn't get it back.

This must be what I deserve.

The day wore on. She rang through to John's office after the students had gone to see whether he wanted to join her for coffee or a late afternoon chat. They would often sit in one or other's office and review the day as a way of getting into the non-work frame of mind. There was no reply. She tried to call Ellie. She hadn't seen her since before the candidate dinner and she had been keen to report back. Ellie's phone went straight through to Sandy who told Anna that he had had a message from Ellie saying she had had to go to Manchester to see her mother who had been taken ill.

I am so selfish. I had no idea Ellie was worried about her mother. I'm just focused on me all the time. That has to change.

She noted to herself that she hadn't really had much contact with Ellie since the first day of term. That was unusual. Even though she had been tied up with the interviewing fiasco, as it now seemed, it was odd that they hadn't grabbed 10 minutes to catch up.

We could always manage to keep each other sane. Just that quick chat. What has happened? What has happened to me?

Anna had lots of work to catch up with particularly after the previous week so she set about it. Essays to mark, management things to respond to and research data to analyze.

Emails kept pinging through to her machine, but she kept focusing on the marking as she knew there would be moans from the students and from the assessment team in the department if she didn't get the grades in on time.

At last she had had done enough and turned to the emails for a mental rest. Anna felt satisfied with most of the students' work.

Thank God! I've done a decent enough job with them.

And she smiled to herself, gratified. She scanned the list of incoming mail, opening several– all the typical content. Students' queries and occasional excuses, emails from colleagues about conferences, research grant applications, minutes from several meetings.

I have too much admin. I need to dump some. It is so bloody boring.

Then she spotted the one email that she was almost coming to expect from **Simon@Little.ac.uk.**

She noted the time it was sent: 4.07 p.m. Just 20 minutes ago.

Ok. What does that man want now?

She read:

I WOULD LOVE TO MEET UP IF YOU HAVE FREE TIME.   S XX

The tone had changed dramatically from the previous one when he bemoaned what he thought she had done to spoil his chances of being appointed as the VC at USEL.

He's trying to confuse me. I won't be drawn in. I bloody won't.

She couldn't focus any more on her backlog of work even so.

I guess I ought to see him. To explain. To make sure he knows I've not done anything against him.

So, she emailed her reply.

WOULD LOVE TO SEE YOU. TOMORROW (Tuesday)? 4 P.M. UNDER THE CLOCK AT WATERLOO?
A

And then after some hesitation she added: 'X'

❋ ❋ ❋

CHAPTER 20

MONDAY EVENING

Anna arrived home. She was absolutely exhausted it was about 6 p.m. – not so late but she had found herself unable to do anything useful in the office. She was also confused. The email exchange had left her feeling positive for the first time since the VC selection shambles.

Why? Is there something that needs to be fixed? Will I manage to fix it when I meet Simon tomorrow?

Dan, as ever, was home standing by the door to welcome her as she walked up the pathway. She saw him there, a smile on his face, his hair tied in the familiar pony tail. He was wearing a tracksuit and holding a towel. Anna guessed he had been for a run and was mopping his face.

'Hi! I just missed a call from your Dorothy Whitaker. It's on the answer machine.'

'She's not *my* Dorothy Whitaker.' They both laughed.

'Actually she sounded a little serious. Said she was on her way over here. Come and listen to the answer machine.'

Anna sighed and followed Dan into the house.

Just when I was beginning to think I might be able to sort things out ....

'What on earth does she want now? I have nothing else to say.'

'Well ...' Dan was standing by the window 'it looks as if you could ask her – here she is now.'

And with that the police inspector pulled her car, a white

Peugeot onto the gravel drive spattering shards of gravel. She was certainly in a hurry.

Anna sighed again touching Dan's hand as she went to open the door. Dorothy who was dressed all in black today climbed out of the car. Her blond hair looked ruffled and her face was pale and drawn. The fashionable clothes and spiked heels that Anna recalled from their previous meeting seemed to belong to a different person. More so someone else was opening the passenger door.

Is this some kind of omen? Don't be so bloody silly.

A man clambered out. He was older than Dorothy, slightly overweight and with grey-streaked brown hair. He too looked careworn. His face, showing what Anna guessed was two-day old stubble, was kind and broke into an easy but weary smile as Dorothy introduced them.

'Anna, Professor Brosnan, this is Detective Sergeant Mallin. Raymond.'

They shook hands and Anna nodded, relieved to see Dan pushing his way forward into the group introducing himself.

I really love the way he looks out for me.

'What might I do for you now?' Anna asked.

'May we go inside?' Raymond Mallin suggested. Dan led the way through the hall into the living room. Just then a car drew up outside and they could hear Alison calling goodbye to her friend Minnie.

Minnie's mum must have driven them home. I wish they would walk!

Dan met Anna's eyes, nodded towards her and went to meet Alison, and Anna guessed, keep her out of the way. The boys were due home a bit later she remembered because of rugby practice.

There was an awkward silence and Anna wondered what was going on. Dan came back.

'She's in the dining room and going to do her homework there. So we're safe for a while' he laughed as he said this but it appeared rather hollow.

They look serious. But they also seem a little uncertain.

'May we all sit down?' this time it was Dorothy's request.

They sat. Anna notice that D.S. Mallin was carrying a buff coloured folder which looked stretched and full. Anna adjusted her position to appear neutral. Sitting straight, but not tense, with her arms resting on her knees, her hands slightly open. *Just as I do when I interview people or counsel distressed students.* That position was not to last for long though.

'Anna. I have some bad news.'

What?

Dorothy continued immediately.

'I'm afraid that Professor Simon Heath was found dead last Thursday night'.

Anna lurched. She felt her mouth fall open. Her eyes suddenly ached. Her pulse went wild and her throat tightened.

'What?' she just about managed.

'He was found at the University of South East London at midnight'.

'Why?' she managed.

'It is a homicide I'm afraid' Mallin added.

'But what was he doing at USEL?'

Dan stood up. He moved towards Anna putting his arm on her shoulder. He looked at Dorothy.

'Please take care. Anna has had too many shocks over the past week. You need to take this slowly and explain. This man is ... well was her enemy. He attacked her. Badly. As you know'.

'We are very sorry to bring this news. But this is now a murder investigation.' And then Dorothy added:

'We would like you to come to the station to answer some questions.'

'What's going on here?' Dan demanded. 'You were here on Friday. You didn't say anything about this then.' He moved away from comforting Anna and faced the two police officers.

'Sir. This is a very serious matter. Please let us do our job.'

Sir?

'Are you arresting Anna?'

'Not right now. No. We need her to help with our inquiries.'

'What have I done?'

'That's what we need to find out.'

A noise at the front door – banging, bell-ringing, laughing and locks opening heralded the earlier than expected arrival of the boys – Anthony and Robert.

'Hi M and D! we're home! No practice tonight' yelled Robert. And then Anthony's voice and the pair burst into the living room.

'We're starving' and then a stunned silence as they were met with the unexpected scene. Dan moved them towards the kitchen.

'Wait' he said to the police officers. 'Let me organize the children before you go any further.'

Anna's mind was racing. So many thoughts were going through her head. But she knew she had to go with the police to try to sort out these events once and for all. When Dan returned to the room looking uncharacteristically tense and flustered Anna said:

'Look it's Ok. This can be sorted. I *need* to have this sorted. Don't worry I shall be fine. I've done nothing. Nothing.'

Anna went into the kitchen as all 3 children looked up nervously.

'I've got to go to London to give some evidence - a murder. Someone I know. … knew.' She immediately wished she hadn't said that as Alison and Robert looked shocked and Anthony grinned.

'Hey that's exciting!'

'It most certainly is not. It was someone I knew a long time ago. It's upsetting. His family must be devastated.'

'Ok'. He said looking down.

'Dad is here. Be good. I shan't be any longer than necessary - but this is all a bit of a mess and the sooner I can tell the cops what I know, the sooner this can be put behind us. Ok guys?'

They all three nodded. Alison had the beginning of tears forming in her eyes. Anna leaned over and kissed them all.

'Won't be long. I promise.'

'Love you mummy' Alison murmured while the boys, now both looking stunned, nodded in agreement.

Anna felt able to leave now, provided no-one said anything else to her.

If they do, I shall scream.

Anna returned to the living room where Dan was oversee-ing the two officers gathering their files - ready to leave. She hugged Dan tightly. He stroked her hair and she felt tears. She patted his back, pulled away and smiling, bravely she thought, followed Dorothy and Raymond out of the house and into the unmarked police Peugeot.

❋ ❋ ❋

CHAPTER 21

MONDAY EVENING

Anna couldn't recall much of the journey to the police station near Waterloo, south of the River Thames, almost directly opposite the Parliament building. They had been driving against the traffic, most of which was heading out of London towards the suburbs at this point in the day. It must have been around or later than 7 p.m. now she thought because the sun, although still bright when they left Endlesham, had faded as they reached their destination. Anna glimpsed the river through the gaps in the new blocks of apartments noticing as if for the first time how the river shone gold and black in the fading light. She wondered faintly whether they would drive her home again after the interview.

Did I bring a jacket? It is cold in the evenings now.

She laughed to herself. Then suddenly she was being helped, or propelled, from the car that Dorothy had parked on a bay by the entrance to the police station. The three of them entered the building - two police detectives and Anna walking between them. As they passed through into the dimly lit entrance lobby Anna blinked. It took a while before she could refocus. There was nothing much to be seen. A dull corridor leading into the distance with doors leading off it on each side. An old counter with stacks of 12 files on shelves wedged behind a tired looking woman with grey hair whose spectacles hung from a chain around her neck.

Subtly, Raymond Mallin guided Anna towards this reception

desk. Somewhere in the distance she heard him tell the female clerk her name and the woman put her spectacles on and pushed a piece of paper towards him. He signed it, handed it back to the woman and nodded to Anna.

Hell! I'm here to be interviewed. Probably a murder suspect. Simon is dead. And I am worried about the cold. What a bastard. He did this to me. Leave me alone bloody Simon. I hate you.

'We'll take your handbag. Don't worry it will be safe.' And she realized she had little choice as she signed another docket that had been pushed across the desk in her direction. Raymond steered her towards, and into, an interview room where she was left alone.

Just like on the TV. But strange. No-one else around now. No 'custody sergeant' or whatever they're called.

She had been left in a room that resembled the seminar rooms in the Psychology Department as USEL. About 10 feet square. Bare, dull off-white painted walls. A table. 4 chairs. She noted that the table and chairs were not chained to the floor something which gave her a slight buzz of optimism. She looked around.

A machine – presumably to record interviews. Ah – and the one-way mirror! Just like the Psych lab.

She wondered if she were being observed even now. Anna recalled something she had heard, although she couldn't recall where or even if it were true.

Guilty people sit still or pretend to go to sleep. Innocent people look anxious. Look around them. Um. What do they think I have done? I could hardly be Simon's killer. Christ! Simon is dead. Is he? Can he be? I only heard from him only this afternoon.

She wondered if that were it – that they had found the messages he had sent.

But then if he was murdered last Thursday night – how could he have emailed me this afternoon? And the email on Friday night? None of this makes sense. I wish they'd bloody hurry up. And we still held an appointment committee meeting on Friday. What's going on?

She looked at her watch.

Damn. I didn't take note of when we arrived. I don't know how long I've been here. Surely too long now. Dan and the kids will be worrying. What can I do?

It wasn't too long before Raymond Mallin came into the interview room followed by Dorothy Whitaker. Mallin turned on the recorder and said who was present.

'We are interviewing you under caution. You have the chance to have a legal representative present. You are not under arrest and as such not obliged to remain in the police station. If you agree to remain you are entitled to free and independent legal advice.'

Anna gulped.

'What does this mean? Do you think I killed Simon?'

'We are investigating the murder of Simon Heath and have reason to believe you might have important information relating to the case.'

'Please get me a lawyer'. She felt weak.

This is not happening.

Mallin handed Anna a form which explained her rights. He told the machine that he had done so, stated the time and then turned it off. As she had never had a reason to engage a lawyer before, other than to buy their house, she was offered the duty solicitor. She waited, again left alone in the interview room, and after 30 minutes or so a man in his late 20s entered the room. He had short, straight ginger hair smoothed down with some kind of moist dressing.

Probably serum. Perhaps his hair is curly. Oh for God's sake woman concentrate. This is not a game now.

The man wore black trousers and a white shirt – both of which looked as if they had been thrown on in haste. He smiled. Henry Robinson, the duty solicitor, made her feel relaxed although she could not fathom the source of that skill. At least not there and then.

Maybe it is simply that he is here for me.

Anna explained her story and particularly that she was totally in the dark about the events that led up to her being here in the police station.

'I do know that I can go home at any time. But I want this sorted. It's nothing to do with me. But I am shocked. I hated the man. No that's not right. I was terrified of him.'

'I am not convinced there is enough evidence to charge you Anna.'

'There can't be *any* evidence surely!' at that point she felt like screaming. 'Please can you get someone to tell me what has happened?'

'I understand that you were exchanging emails, and I believe some friendly postcards, with Mr. Heath.' He paused and looked at her. Anna felt that her mouth was hanging open wanting the next piece of information because she still hadn't a clue as to what was going on.

'And I also understand that you had been expecting to meet with him tomorrow.'

'Yes!' she was screaming now. 'Yes. I was. But he's dead. He's dead. I'm told he has been dead since Thursday night'.

Suddenly she felt as if she had been punched in the stomach. She doubled up in real physical pain. The past 20 years of holding herself together seemed to be unravelling in front of this man. Her pain from the past hurt so much more than the fear of being here in the police station. She was glad he was dead. The tears began to fall.

Maybe now I can reclaim myself. *Purge that man from my mind. My body. I can still feel him. It makes me sick. I make me sick.*

Anna rocked in the chair. Back and forth as if that movement were able to cleanse the memory. The feeling. Pain and shame. She clenched her arms across her stomach holding onto her elbows. She realized she was pinching her upper arms. Pushing the tips of her fingers into her flesh. It hurt but if was also a comfort. She started to sob once again faintly aware that her whole body was shaking with each sob. She stopped rocking. She tried to sit up straight in the chair but her stomach hurt so much that she had to continue to hold it.

Hold yourself together. Keep a grip.
So many thoughts were flooding into her mind. That night with her friends. The inebriation. She had been out of control. The pain.
Had they all been out of control? I hang on to that excuse. Control. Not my fault. Was it just me?
She shivered.
The other person who had been there.
She was now unaware of anyone else in the room even though the man with the ginger hair must still have been present. She found herself clutching at her chest. Scratching her breast-bone. Pushing something down in her mind. Down. Down. Earlier memories. Anxieties. Feelings that couldn't be described. Not words - images. Physical pain. Waves of nausea.
'Anna? Are you Ok?'
The stupid question brought her back to the present. She looked up. Her hair was wet across her face. And her tears continued to fall but there was no momentum now. The tears were a habit.
From long ago? From the last few moments?
Raymond Mallin re-entered the room. Anna thought that he had been watching her. She was embarrassed but somehow felt stronger than she had done for some years.
How odd?
'Do you have any further questions for my client?' Henry asked.
'We are sorry to have had to put you through this. But I suggest you return home now. One of our sergeants will drive you. We may need to ask you more questions. You're no longer a suspect.'
Anna stared. At Henry her solicitor and at Raymond Mallin the detective sergeant who had hardly touched the surface of questions she might have expected. But there were answers she wanted.
'What has happened to Simon? I want to know?'
'We are unsure as yet. But we shall be keeping his family in-

formed. We shall also be updating your Vice-Chancellor, Professor Fielding.'

* * *

CHAPTER 22

TUESDAY

Anna found it difficult to wake herself even as the bright sunlight squeezed its way through the gap in the curtains. She reluctantly opened her eyes. She looked around for Dan finding only the ruffled duvet. She felt the place where he should have been. It was still warm. She sat up in bed feeling a little safer. He was the only person who could provide her with any comfort and restore her soul. Shortly Dan, ever solicitous, came quietly into the bedroom with 2 cups of tea and clambered into bed next to her. He smiled and kissed her gently on the forehead balancing her mug of tea in his right hand. They laughed as she managed to take it without either of them spilling a drop. She immediately began to feel a little better.

'What happened yesterday?' even as she asked this Anna thought it was Dan who should be asking.

'Take it slowly. It will come back to you and we can talk about it all as much as you want to. But for now – one thing at a time.'

It was too much to take in. Simon was dead. Apparently murdered.

But was he really dead before sending emails? Had he put a delay on them? Was it someone else sending them? Was he really alive and an elaborate game was being played against me?

Anna couldn't face the children right now. She could hardly face herself without Dan. She experienced a terrible shame that the children had seen the police take her away, even if she hadn't been arrested. Even if she had been brought home with no charges. But for some reason she felt guilty. A sense of personal badness. And then she remembered how support from her colleagues had evaporated when she might have needed them the most. She remembered Ellie who had problems of her own that Anna had not known. But Gabriel and Donald – perhaps even John. They had not been there for her and Donald was almost hostile. Why?

Should I call in sick? Cancel my lecture? The tutorials?

Anna's world was imploding. The shock of Simon's return to her consciousness. To her life. The man whose existence she had pushed away. When she met Dan, she thought she had succeeded in burying what Simon had done to her. It had been hard to look after herself following that vicious rape. It was several years later before Anna could actually name it. She remembered how she couldn't face going into the university where she and her friends were studying for their doctorates in case she would see Simon. And she couldn't even go there now. It was just across the river from the USEL campus and often there were interesting guest speakers, sought after library books and friends working and studying there. But even after all these years she could not face crossing the bridge and entering those buildings. Just in case he would be there. Or at least memories of him.

Silly fool. But he's gone now.

But she couldn't help herself. The pain had been real then and had returned. It had not healed. She thought it had but now she knew.

I should have faced it then. Sought help. I was a coward.

'I think I know how you feel today Anna, but if you can bear it you should go to work even if you leave early to come home.' The gentle voice intruded into the self-persecution.

Anna resolved not to see herself as a coward any more. She was going in to work. She was going to sort out the children and get them ready for school. She was going to heal.

Easier said than done but I have survived.

The boys were still in their bedroom – Robert staring at his iPad and Anthony shuffling through a pile of books and papers scattered around the floor.

'Come on you two what's going on now?'

'Mum. I can't find last night's homework. He's lost it' Anthony pointed at Robert. His face began to crumble. Anna grabbed him and held him to her. Robert seemed oblivious to any activity in the room. Anna strode over to his bed and whipped the iPad away.

'Mum! No!'

'Come on now both of you. Who's having the first shower?'

Robert stormed out into the general direction of the family bathroom. Anthony, the more gentle soul of the pair, looked at Anna.

'Mum what happened with the police? I really thought I would never see you again.' And he was close to tears.

'Nothing is going to take me away from you. From any of you' and she hugged him once again. 'A man I used to work with – before I met dad. Well he … he is dead. The police think he was murdered.'

'You didn't do it?'

'Hell no. Of course not. But the police wanted to talk to everyone they thought might know him. And about him.' Then softly: 'He wasn't very nice. I didn't like him'.

'Have you ironed my blouse? You haven't. You don't care.' Alison burst into the boys' bedroom.

'Actually there is a freshly ironed blouse waiting for you in your wardrobe. Try looking!' Anna felt a wave of guilt. She was being horrible to Alison. But teenage girls were a pain and Anna was not in the mood to apologize or tackle Alison who had already stormed out. She could hear the wardrobe door banging and the sound of something being pulled from a coat hanger.

Naturally Dan came to the rescue and suggested that he take over for now. Anna, consumed with gratitude, refocused her efforts on getting herself ready to face the world of USEL.

BELIEVE ME

* * *

CHAPTER 23

Anna peered through the bedroom window to check on the weather.

The sky was still bright blue but now with a cold-looking edge. She needed to get dressed and catch the 8.15 train. She pondered on which coat to wear over her blue skinny jeans and blue linen blouse. These were among her favourite clothes – the ones that made her feel most comfortable and like herself. The suits and stylish shoes that characterized the formality of the previous week had left her feeling something of a fraud. They were definitely not her style.

Deciding that there would be no rain that day she chose her black leather jacket. It was strange how important clothes could be for a person's mood and motivation. This was Anna's version of power dressing and she felt she could cope with whatever the day chose to throw at her – and she knew it would be throwing something!

A good choice. I am ready to fight if I have to!

'Bye everyone – where are you?' She called as she descended into the hallway. All four of her family emerged from the kitchen and she kissed them all goodbye feeling slightly uplifted.

Although heaven knows why.

She walked down the short, graveled drive and headed to the station determined to enjoy the walk, the weather and the thought of the lecture – one of her favourites – that she had recently updated.

Social influence and the role of the bystander.

The now infamous experiments in social psychology conducted during the middle of the previous century had con-
temporary resonance. Now it was not just that ordinary
people obeyed those in authority or didn't come to the aid of
people in trouble as in psychology's famous examples; bully-
ing and humiliation via social media was rife. But did anyone
care? Children and adults could be made to feel small and
worthless and in severe cases made to self-harm and even kill
themselves. And many of these horrendous events had thou-
sands of silent witnesses. This topic invariably encouraged
her students to think and argue about the psychological basis
of these behaviours. As they became excited - so did she.

That's why I do this job.

Anna felt herself smiling as she walked along the familiar
road when suddenly she heard the screeching of car breaks
too nearby for comfort. She turned suddenly to see a bright
red Mini skidding to a halt. The driver's door flung open and a
fair-haired young woman called out:

'Professor Brosnan?'

Anna stopped in her tracks not recognizing the woman. A
sudden terror gripped her.

Is it Dan? The children? Christ.

She began to tremble with the optimistic mood a distant
memory.

'What's the matter?' she felt herself stuttering.

'Sue Abbott. *London Daily Argus'* the woman screamed at her.
Or so it seemed.

'Oh' was all Anna could think to say then 'What can I do for
you?'

'Interview' the woman was out of breath but was now standing in front of Anna blocking her way.

'I'm going to catch a train now.'

'I'll drive you. All the way.'

Anna felt bemused.

Well why not. She looks harmless enough.
'Well Ok. But what do you want to talk to me about exactly?'
'Your arrest for the murder of Simon Heath.' Then under her breath: 'of course. What else?'
'Bloody hell. Don't be stupid. I've not been arrested. And I have no idea if Professor Heath was murdered. And you need to know if he has been murdered – it wasn't me.' She almost wanted to punch this woman. Anna didn't know where that violent anger had come from, but it helped her push the woman out of her way and stride on towards the station.
'So I can quote you on that then?' called the indefatigable Sue Heath as she watched Anna retreat from her grasp.
Anna reached the station – small, familiar and generally providing a sense of belonging and community. But not so today. Anna saw her train leaving the platform. She would have to wait another 20 minutes which meant she would have to go immediately to give her lecture.
No chat. No coffee. Damn.
The platform was almost empty now as most of the regular commuters had caught the last train due to arrive in London before 9 a.m. Clouds were forming leaving an intermittent pale warmth. She shivered, questioning whether the chill came from inside or out. She looked around and then chose a seat on one of the benches inside a shelter and settled down to wait.
She thought about the retreating journalist who may or may not print her shouted denial of murder. It would have been hilarious if it had not been such a nightmare. Anna's mind drifted. She started to think back to Simon and what he had done to her. Not only the violent rape, but her sense that she had to hide from him. Anna shuddered again.
That I was the one who should feel shame. He should have been scared of me.
But the impact of what she had gone through made it impossible for her to think so at the time. Then, as she recovered at home and working in the bookshop which had proven to

be fun after a while, she learned to bury her emotions. And to bury those memories. She chose somewhere new to restart her career. And she was a success. A relatively young female professor. She was near to top of her trade and she knew she had done this without the assistance of a mentor or an old boys' network'.

Come on – pat yourself on the back occasionally.

But it was hard. She thought about how the reappearance of Simon had led to an intense physical reaction as well as the emotion. There was also that strange ambiguity – he had seemed to want to reconnect with her. He had not appeared to recognize how he had attacked her life. It was not just her body. One unforgiveable upshot of what had happened was that she lost contact with her former friends and fellow doctoral students. She had been pulled out of the professional race.

In one way it had been her intention to avoid the shame by keeping quiet about the attack. She knew that Tina and Michelle had been interested in Simon and would have been envious that she had lured him to her flat. That thought made her feel sick. And more so, she herself had fancied him. It was unbearable. But now? Now he was dead and the events surrounding his death were unclear. And there was still a lurking anxiety that she was being blamed, or framed, for what happened. Anna resolved to try to discover more about Simon. His life and his death. Had he raped and abused others who might have sought revenge in a way that she had never countenanced? She became lost in these thoughts when the announcement predicted that her train would arrive on time five minutes hence.

❊ ❊ ❊

CHAPTER 24

Anna quickly found a seat on this later train.

She eased herself next to the window, grateful that for once there was no-one bumping or pushing into her. She rolled her head back staring at the ceiling of the carriage in an attempt to relax and clear her mind. She particularly wanted to forget that journalist. She also wanted to forget her experience at the police station. And to forget – or at least work out – what had happened with Simon. The last few whirlwind days. She thought about how lucky she was to have had such unwavering support from Dan despite her belief that she should have confessed to him about the rape several years ago.

Why do I think it was a 'confession?' I was the victim. But maybe I wasn't so innocent. Was it my fault?

She wondered whether she could have survived without Dan. He was kind, solicitous and knew how to remove every-day burdens. He was great with the kids too. He had to be right now. Anna still couldn't make sense of Simon's recent re-entry into her life. And then his death.

The earlier clouds had moved to reveal a bright blue blinding sunshine piercing the carriage windows. Anna closed her eyes briefly feeling pleased with the world. She sank into thought. She intended to think about Simon, but her mind kept drawing her back to Dan.

Anna's early life with Dan had been far from comfortable, despite the way the couple appeared now to their friends and family. He had been the manager of the bookstore in the Suffolk market town where she had worked following her flight from Simon, her friends and London. Dan appeared uncomplicated, unambitious and generous accepting her for who she wanted to be at that point – a graduate student taking a break from studies. He was a few years older than her, a newcomer to the area where Anna had been born and where her parents had lived all of her life. Basically, this town was where she called 'home'.

She was immediately drawn to Dan's blue-grey eyes that sparkled whenever he looked at her and his long straight brown hair, frequently contained in a pony tail. He reminded her of an artist or musician. But whatever he might have been, she considered he was one of a kind. She liked that.

Gradually as the weeks and months passed they lingered together at the end of the working day and eventually Anna plucked up the courage to invite him for a drink. He accepted. They became close friends. As the academic year wore on, Anna knew she had to apply for doctoral studies at another university and was delighted to be accepted at the University of Norwich. From there she could live at home with her parents and see Dan. He had become her lover and before too long, he was her husband. They married after she was awarded her doctorate, soon after which she was appointed to a lectureship at the USEL. And then, with her parents' help, they bought their house in Endlesham – easy commuting distance to London. Then along came Alison followed by the boys.

But that wasn't exactly how it happened. It's never that straightforward.

Anna's parents seemed to like Dan, although they were unhappy that their high-flying daughter could settle for a seemingly unambitious book-shop manager. Anna became angry each time this issue came between them. She loved Dan. Looking back though she asked herself how much it was his laidback attitude that attracted her at a time when she was recovering from the pressure of London, her PhD and Simon. Dan had talked about why he was apparently so content with a job punching below his weight. His explanation, if he had needed one, had always been:

'I'm just a hippy a few decades too late'.

And then he would laugh and put his arms around her. She knew he loved to read, to draw and listen to music. He didn't have too many friends from his past, but customers of the book store frequently sought him out for advice and a chat. He could play the guitar and sing reasonably well with an occasional appearance in one of the local pubs when they had 'open mike' nights. Dan seemed content with this and as a consequence, so did Anna. Dan was not going to compete with her. Dan was more than happy to support her as the main bread-winner once they had news of the USEL appointment. Anna was surprised, but secretly delighted that he was agreeable to leaving Suffolk, and the book shop, with no obvious regrets.

He's worked here so long. And yet he is prepared to move at the drop of a hat for me and my career.

Anna thought she had discovered the perfect husband. And, in many ways, she had and he continued to be so. One day shortly after they moved to Endlesham, Dan was out for his morning run when a large bundle of re-directed mail arrived through their front door. This was an assorted bunch of envelopes – different shapes, sizes, shades, typed and written addresses. Perfectly normal. All from different people. There was only one thing they had in common that shocked Anna as she sorted through them. All were addressed to *Dr.* Daniel Brosnan.

Doctor? Does Dan have a PhD? Or is this a mistake – are they for me?

She had to wait until she had returned from work to ask him about it. She was anxious as she didn't know what his excuse would be.

And I assumed an excuse. How reprehensible I am.

He told her. He was a qualified medical doctor – a general practitioner. He had worked for two or three years after leaving university in Yorkshire – long enough to gain his postgraduate license in general practice.

'But something awful happened to me.' She saw his eyes darken and tears form. He rubbed his neck and passed a hand under his eyes. He gained a little strength then, enough to look directly at her.

Anna felt she was accusing him of something dreadful even though, after her initial surprise, she was motivated mostly by curiosity.

'I was convicted of dangerous driving.'

'Oh' Anna couldn't work out the connection. She continued to stare at him waiting for more explanation. At first he looked as if he had finished explaining although nothing yet made sense.

'I don't understand what that has to do with you being a doctor?'

I might as push him further even if the explanation is painful. We have to clear the air.

'Yeh. Well. Ok. My friends and I had been out for a drink. Out in the Peak District.'

Anna looked shocked.

'No. No I wasn't drunk but I had had a pint. No more than that. I was going to be the driver, so I was very careful. The others became raucous and I sensed they were verging on the abusive. We were all a bit rough as medical students. Rugby culture and all that. But most of us got over that once we were doing our house jobs. But not Tom. Not really.'

Anna nodded urging him to go on.

'So.' He hesitated. He blew bits of stray hair off his face and tugged at his pony tail. He sniffed.

Is he crying?

'Tom, one of our crowd – bloody typical. Planning to be a surgeon. His father a local magistrate.' He then sniffed again and ran his hand under his nose. 'He started chatting up this woman. Tom did. About our age. But a local Derbyshire girl. With a man. Her bloke you know?' Anna nodded although she didn't really know.

'The man. Well he was big. Tough looking. Blue collar.' Then Dan began shaking with the memory and put his face into his hands. He couldn't look at her or anything else. She had never known Dan to be anything other than her rock and awareness that he could be shattered was alarming. She tried to ignore that feeling and moved nearer to him. She grabbed his hands, kissing them, and then she kissed his face. It was wet. He looked at her and she could see he was weeping openly now. *What could have happened. This is terrible for him.*

'Please go on. It will help I'm sure'.

'Psychologist!' he said and smiled at her through his obvious pain. 'Well. I pulled Tom away and out of the pub. The landlord followed us out and thanked me. Gareth and Martin – the other two – were pissed. Not incapable but pretty bloody drunk. I was getting angry. They were no help and Tom was rat-arsed. He kept pulling away from me trying to return to the pub. The landlord was good. He stayed and made sure we were far enough away from the entrance that Tom wouldn't be going back'.

Anna looked at him. She had never seen Dan this distressed ever before.

'So. Maybe you can guess?'

'No. Not really – what happened. Please tell me.'

'Well. I got Tom into the front seat and buckled him up.' Anna smiled. 'Gareth and Martin got themselves into my car. Martin then threw up in the back seat ....'

'Ugh!' from Anna.

'Yeh. Well. Definitely. But as I drove off – out of the car park of the pub. It was slightly elevated. Above the main road. Trees around it.'

'Yes?'

'The woman from the pub – the one Tom had been interested in - was walking across the car park, down a slope to the road.

There was no pavement – country road you see?'

'Um.'

'I drove slowly all the time smelling the bloody vomit. I felt sick. I was also furious. Bloody furious with all of them. The all of a sudden Tom spots the woman. He tries to take the belt off to jump out of the car. I swerve and try to speed up to get out of there before he causes trouble. But he manages to get out of the car anyway.'

'Blimey. That is scary.'

'Yes. For sure it was. Tom fell out leaving the door open and pulled at it to keep his balance. I was seriously scared. I put my foot on the break, but by then he had got hold of the woman. Physically pulled her onto the ground and the car hit her head. *I hit her head with the car I was driving*. That's the truth of it.'

'Oh God. How awful. For her. You.'

'So. She is dead. Ambulances. Police. All the usual. I was prosecuted. Got a suspended prison sentence. Tom's father had some influence. I could have gone to jail but of course he knew – or at least guessed – a version of what really had happened. I don't think I shall ever get over it. I was also suspended by the GMC – General Medical Council ...'

'Yeh. I know.'

'Apparently so-called 'alcohol related' suspensions are reasonably common. So is reinstatement. I was suspended for 6 months. Then I could return to my postgrad training. I applied for my next house job in Suffolk. I knew Tom and the others had opted for far sexier places – Glasgow, York and London. Medically Suffolk's a bit of a dump. Sorry!' Dan smiled weakly.

'But I couldn't cope any more. I worked for a while in Ipswich – I did the full 6 months and passed the assessments, but all the time I felt ... not sure how to describe it. Kind of *shaky*. That's it really. Then I saw the advert for the book shop manager – well I was happy. Then *we* met and I was even happier.'

Anna grabbed his hand and stroked it. He squeezed her hand

and moved away. She remembered how his head turned from her as he stood up and moved to the kitchen. They had not discussed this again.

But why not? He needs to resolve those feelings. Is there anything more?

She dismissed those thoughts.

The train was well on its way to Waterloo by the time she had finished deliberating. She felt a sense of shame. She had known for many years now about Dan's secret. His life trauma. But she had only told him hers when forced to.

Or is that fair? I had to ask about those letters.

They had left Clapham Junction behind. The train was full now. The majority of passengers were standing in the aisle between the rows of seats. Anna was pleased she had a window seat and could look out at the skyline. The landmark buildings of the Shard and the Razor in the near distance stood out above pre-Victorian churches and shabby streets with their dilapidated shops. She then looked to the left, through the gaps between her standing travelling companions. The view to that side had always been the Parliament buildings and the River Thames. But these landmarks had become partly obscured by clusters of half-built apartment blocks peppered with the occasional glimpse of ageing public housing and Lambeth Palace, the official London home of the Archbishop of Canterbury. Anna sighed.

Everything changes.

The train predictably ground to a halt a few yards before the platform trapping the eager commuters in the carriage. Surprisingly it started up again almost immediately jolting the standing travellers as they reached the platform. Anna suddenly landed back on earth. She climbed out of the carriage and moved slowly, in step with the others towards the ticket barrier.

What surprises was this day going to hold?

❖ ❖ ❖

CHAPTER 25

Were there going to be journalists waiting at the University?

In some ways it made more sense for them to be at the scene of the alleged crime than pursuing her through the suburbs. Simon had died on campus – or so she had been told. *Could that really be true? What was he doing at USEL? After the dinner presumably?*

Nothing was making sense anymore. It was still only Tuesday. It then hit her – the day she had planned to meet him after work. But the email arranging the meeting had arrived after he was supposed to have died.

Supposed to? Of course he died. But last Thursday? The police were not going to pretend about something like this.

She left Waterloo Station behind her as usual. Out through the vaulted main exit, carefully crossing the roads where taxis and buses fought with commuters and headed towards the double archway at the busy southern side of Waterloo Bridge, picking up a *City Extra* along the way. The exhaust fumes seemed overwhelming today and Anna noticed a yellow mist masking the chilly blue sky. Coming from all sides now were reassuring bunches of students in crocodile formations. Some of them were familiar and nodded politely as she overtook them. She smiled feeling warmer towards the day ahead.

She knew that Gabriel would have arrived on the earlier

train. She also knew that she needed to keep walking at her fast pace if she were to be in the lecture theatre on time.

And without being sweaty and panting.

As she entered the campus, she quickened her stride to avoid glancing around – she didn't want to have to strike up a conversation or make excuses as to why she had to run. She reached her office, grabbed the memory stick with the lecture power-point and, without the benefit of a coffee, decided to set up her presentation slides in the theatre. One or two students were scattered in seats across the lecture hall – some in small groups chatting others looking at their phones. Typically they ignored her arrival so she set to work with the computer and projector unhindered. The equipment was good enough that it was only rarely that one had to call for technical assistance these days.

She pulled the memory stick from her bag.

That's odd – I thought I had put this lecture on the pink flash drive.

And then she remembered.

Sandy's memory stick of course.

She dived into her bag once again and pulled out the pink one with the relevant presentation. But she perceived her heart beginning to pound and she was sweating. In the moment she had totally forgotten the present state of affairs.

How had I failed to check Sandy's flash drive?

It didn't take a great deal of effort to recall the events of the previous day.

My God. What the Hell has happened to me? To Simon? OK now focus. Social influence and the role of the bystander! That's all I need to think about over the next hour. Hoorah!

It wasn't hard to do. She loved this part of her job. A show off? Yes - she probably was but most academics were like that so she didn't distinguish herself in that respect. It was a necessary, but unacknowledged, component of their work.

She looked up and there they were – a lecture theatre almost full. Stragglers entering from the door behind her and from the back of the lecture theatre.

'Good morning everyone.'

And she received a greeting from the assembled group. Pens, papers, recording devices, usually phones, were on the benches in front of them and around 70% looked up expectantly. Those who didn't were reasonably quiet, so she glanced at the large clock face on the far wall and started the lecture. Initially she outlined the programme details for the term ahead, gave hand-outs to the students at each end of the front bench to pass around. Then she flicked on her first power point.

50 minutes later she was packing up her notes and gathering the left-over handouts, unplugging her flash drive while half listening and responding to the inevitable group of 5 or 6 people who had individual questions about what had just been discussed or what was to come. And, naturally, one person had a reason that they wouldn't be handing their essays in on time. She checked the desk and the lectern to ensure she hadn't left anything and then groped in her bag to make sure she had both flash drives. She nodded her farewell to the remaining students who were still milling around. An unconscious message that she was done there. They'd have to wait for next time if they had other questions.

Now to relax a little. The first coffee of the day.

Anna thought she might go to the staff canteen where she was able to get a good quality cappuccino. She could do with a biscuit as well. The canteen was at the opposite end of the main building from the Psychology Department but almost immediately above the main theatre where she had just finished her lecture. Psychology was a particularly popular subject and consequently most of the lectures were held in that theatre – the one with the greatest capacity.

This was the first time since the previous spring that she had delivered a large lecture. By the time the summer term arrived students had had the bulk of new material so that became revision time. It was no surprise then to Anna that she felt a mixture of exhilaration following the students' obvious enjoyment of the session while being depleted from the renewed effort involved. Her voice was strained too but she was happy.

This is what I do!

There was only a short queue for coffee and biscuits – most people had finished their morning break, but it was too early for lunch. She found a table easily, opened the biscuit packet and stared around her. The canteen had large tinted windows that overlooked one of the many railway arches around Waterloo. She stared at the slow-moving trains aware even through the tinted glass, that the bright misty day had now changed into one with low slung yellow clouds.

As she processed her thoughts about the gloomy weather she, along with the deliberations and chatter of all the others in the canteen, was interrupted by a loud clatter and flash of lights. She dropped her biscuit and jogged her coffee cup spilling some of it.

Bugger.

A man's voice was calling out 'Professor Brosnan? Professor Brosnan?' and then from a woman:

'Anna – are you here?' followed by a cacophony of voices – female and male all of different strengths and tones.

By this time around seven people had pushed their way into the canteen, some holding microphones attached to what she guessed were portable recording machines and others with cameras which flashed on and off unremittingly. Some of her colleagues in the canteen stared in shock at the newcomers while others, who knew who she was, stared at her. It was obvious to the reporters now that they were seeking the woman with the curly red hair holding a biscuit and staring at them in astonishment.

'Anna. Anna. *The Daily Mirror*. Please may I talk to you?'

'BBC news – we are investigating Professor Heath's murder. You can tell your side of the story.'

'*The Evening Standard* Professor. What happened to your friend Simon Heath? Is it true you were having a relationship with him?'

'*The Telegraph*. What can you tell us about his murder? Why were you held by the police?'

'Anna. Anna. ITV news. We want an exclusive. Give your side. Did you do it?'

'*The Guardian*. I understand Professor Heath was an activist for women's rights in higher education? Was that why he was murdered?'

By then they had swooped around her – some had pulled up chairs. Others were simply thrusting cameras and microphones at her face from a standing position. Anna wanted to scream at them. She also felt helpless.

What do I do? What can I do?

Fortunately, a loud male voice that turned out to belong to Ian Fielding the interim VC, bellowed at the intruders telling them that no interviews would be permitted until they had met with the university's public relations department.

He is definitely forceful. Powerful. Thank God.

Anna prepared herself for what might be coming her way later in the day. She managed to finish the coffee and biscuit and headed for her office watching carefully for signs of a further media onslaught. She was amazed but there was no evidence that anything out of the ordinary had happened. Students and staff roamed the corridors and only those she knew well exchanged nodded greetings with her.

CHAPTER 26

Anna knew she had to find out whatever Sandy had recorded on the flash drive.

I don't understand what all this surreptitious electronic spying in the department is about. What have we got to hide? And who cares anyway?

That was the real issue. Anna tried to think logically. If Shirley routinely went to the trouble of placing secret recording and video equipment around the departmental offices, and who knew wherever else, there had to be a reason beyond mere curiosity. Was something weird going on here? Something that Anna was oblivious to?

Although curiosity is a strong motivator sometimes. Well yes if there is something interesting happening. But what on earth is interesting about the departmental office? It's mostly about students, teaching hours ..... um I know she moans about having too much teaching – ha ha! Doesn't she just! And well, sex I guess, but I've not seen much of this until ..... shit. Bloody bitch. Calm down. Calm down.

Anna resolved to do some serious investigation about events resulting from the dark roller-coaster of recent days. A death. Memories of assault, violence and her own sense of blame. The time she had failed her husband – not telling him about the rape. But also, not really knowing who he was until they were married. Had *he* failed *her*?

Everyone has secrets. Not everyone tries to trap people into re-

vealing them. Is Shirley blackmailing someone? Is that what it is about? And who?

Anna sat at her desk staring at her computer as it booted up. She held the flash drive in her hand, slowly and thoughtfully twisting it around. She stood up and walked to the office door and locked it. Something she had never done before. Now she felt slightly safer. By then the computer screen had calmed down declaring that Word, Excel, Outlook and PowerPoint had been updated. The desktop picture showed Dan standing behind the boys with Alison and Anna each side of him. They were all smiling.

The perfect family.

She had been so used to seeing that photo on the screen that she rarely gave it more than a second glance and definitely no thought.

Are we so perfect?

She wondered. Anna looked again at the image on the screen. She looked serene. Not now though. She took a deep breath and placed the memory stick into the port at the back of the hard drive. A list of 2 folders appeared. One with an icon resembling a loud speaker and another indicating a video. She tapped her key to open the audio folder. She pressed play on the first audio file. She noted the time and date. The date was three weeks ago towards the end of the summer vacation and the time was 22.30.

My goodness what on earth would be going on at that time of night during the student vacation? Would it be the cleaners?

It was difficult to make out what was being said, even at full volume, because the printer or the photocopier had been churning away in the background when the recording took place. What Anna thought she could hear however shattered her sense of normality. She could make out both Donald Delaney's and John Jones' voices. She was almost 100% certain it was them. Her friends. They were arguing. Anna could discern enough of what was being said to form an impression – even a theory. She made notes as she listened.

You know what happened/ had been (John – apparently angry – at least loud and almost shrill). You were to blame. You've caused this. …. In danger (sounded as if …)
Mumble – yes. (Donald? – I think it must be him)
How could you live with it/him/? You are a total bastard (John)
What (something) you gone/done? Not the only one am I? (Donald)
It was a shitty …….her/fur/ (John)
You need to bloody well sort this out before/or I get Jonah/Joanna seen to / been to (Donald)
Fuck off (John)
You'll hear more/all before I know/go down. He'll take you too (Donald)

She was shocked. It was strange when people you knew so well had conversations that didn't fit into the picture you had of them and their relationship. As far as Anna had been aware until this point Donald and John rarely gave each other a thought. Nor had she imagined that they would have anything to say to each other about work or private matters.
How can people I know have lives without me knowing? And late at night in the office? Maybe Shirley has a point! There are things going on that none of us knows about. But what could make John so angry – he's the ultimate Mr. Relaxed. The 'John Jones approach'.

The conversation went on:

She's your friend/a bend/lend. (Donald – yes it is definitely him!)

Or even 'round the bend'. Get a grip on yourself woman I don't think this is a laughing matter.

And you have always behaved as. …… be/she as well (John)
Indecipherable loud voice – door banging.
Shuffling and continued churning of the photocopier/printer.

I have to guess that someone stormed out at that point. Also, presumably this is voice activated so nothing more – I guess the printer noise doesn't register.

Anna sat at her desk staring at her notes adding further comments.

John is angry with Donald. He thinks Donald has harmed someone. Possibly a 'she'.
John thinks Donald should be ashamed. But John is worried about something he had done. Being threatened?
Donald has possibly betrayed/spied on or something to a friend of his and/or John's.
Shirley?
Me????
What has Donald done? What has it to do with John? What has John done? Is it Joanna they refer to? Perhaps this is a matter for HR? Shirley again?

She felt strangely calm. It was a little like a game. Or more so deciphering the meaning of data from a research project. There was a mystery here and she figured that there might be a connection with Simon. And perhaps Simon's death. *Although I am unsure why I should think that encounter had anything to do with what has happened. It all took place weeks before he was even relevant to us here at USEL.* But instinctively she knew there was something.

But maybe people knew that Adrian would be leaving suddenly and Simon might replace him? And I need to talk to Sandy. He knows something. Well he must do – he's downloaded this stuff from the spy devices.

Anna sat thinking some more but couldn't get beyond her intuition at this stage. She also recognized that she was hardly going to be objective. Donald was indeed her friend – but he had been behaving abnormally over the past few days. John was definitely her friend but even he had been a bit remote since the Simon stuff.

Are they talking about me? And what on earth could they find to argue about?

She glanced at the second icon – the video. With some trepidation she pressed the button to watch.

The picture flickered onto the screen. It then became calm as a clear black and white scene of the main departmental office appeared. Sandy's desk with his 2 adjacent PCs facing her in the foreground. The desk where the two part-time secretaries would take it in turns to sit a few feet in front to the right of Sandy. The metal stationery cupboard taking up the length of wall next to the door out to the corridor near to Anna's office. She shuddered. Nothing seemed to be happening though. The date on the screen showed the first day of term, last Monday – the first day of term, at 07.30.

Then the office door opened inwards – there was a slight creak so just a little sound - and Shirley walked in. She was wearing her coat and carrying her handbag and briefcase. She looked around plonking the case on the vacant secretarial desk and her handbag on the floor next to it. She looked at her watch. She loosened her coat and perched herself on the desk, looking again at her watch. Nothing else happened. She stood up and looked to the side of the stationery cupboard.

That's one of the places that she had placed a bug!

She peered around the cupboard and reached out her arm feeling for something. She brought her arm back slowly, apparently satisfied.

The recorder must still be in place.

Then Anna wondered:

Where is this camera? It must be above the window behind Sandy. Yes! there it will get a view of the whole room – nothing hidden. I can see that. A panorama.

Shirley raised herself up looked again at her watch and began to pace. Then the door opened. Simon, wearing a coat and beret entered. Shirley walked up to him – she was very near. But they didn't hug. Shirley was shouting at him. Anna could hear a few words – she made some notes.

.... Wife ...what will she do? (from Shirley)
I don't care. You won't (that was clear from Simon).

Shirley turned her back to him which meant she was more or less facing the camera.
Face like thunder.
Itch. Bitch?

Shirley turned around to face him. Simon looked distraught which surprised Anna. That was not how she recalled ever seeing him.

What you did .....then.....tell her. .....Donald knows/closed/goes.

Anna then remembered, and it seemed so long ago now, that Donald had been very positive about the possibility of Simon becoming VC. She had thought it odd, but Donald had given academic reasons which Anna had noted and considered. But events had most definitely taken over from former gossip and chatting.

But there is a connection. One between Simon, Shirley and Donald. And maybe even John? I would hardly have believed it if someone had said that two weeks ago. But now? I really need to dig further.

Just then a knock on the door caused Anna to jump up from her seat. She nearly called out with her characteristic, lazy 'come in' but with a start she remembered she had locked herself in. She leapt up to unlock and open the door. Something had made her want to protect her territory. And her computer. And herself.

CHAPTER 27

Anna was taken aback to find the journalist Sue Abbott entering her room.

She appeared a lot less frantic than when she had accosted Anna earlier that day, making her miss her train.

'I am sorry about this morning Professor Brosnan'.

Anna looked hard at her visitor, attempting to assess her demeanor, admitting to herself that the woman did appear genuinely concerned. And contrite. She was young. Or at least Anna guessed she was slightly under 30. She wore her fair hair short and swept back off her forehead and behind her ears, although several strands had slithered forward. Her eyelids were emphasized by faint green eyeshadow with a little mascara. Her fitted yellow woolen dress was topped by a black jacket while, unusually, her black shoes had almost flat heels.

Not what you expect of a power-dressing journalist but then ....
How else might you chase after your prey?

Anna smiled to herself.

'Ok. Sit down please do. I am kind of busy right now - so what may I do for you?' Anna felt it best to play gently.

'Professor …'.

'Anna, please.'

'Thank you – er Anna.'

'So?'

'I have information. On the death – rather murder - of your

friend Professor Heath. And I can prove you didn't do it!'
Anna wanted to tell this woman that Simon Heath was no friend of hers but held the feelings back. She wanted to tell her that she herself did actually *know* she hadn't done it – but that seemed silly. Anna needed to discover what this was all about. It seemed to Anna that she was the last to realize anything despite the emotional drama she had been put through over the last few days. And those days felt like a life time.
'Please go on Sue. May I call you that – I recall that is the name you told me?' Anna hesitated to say more but kept watch. The woman looked relaxed but eager. She managed to meet Anna's eyes without attempting to stare her out.
This woman appears genuine but what does she want in return for whatever information?
'It is. Yes. Well. I …. Have a friend. Yes. Friend.'
So do I. Bloody get on with this.
'Well no. My partner. Wife'.
Wife? Oh. I see.
Anna nodded.
'A long time ago. She was a student at the LSSPS – you know the London School for Social and Psychological Sciences?'
This was a hammer blow to Anna.
God. What now. Who? What is she going to tell me?
'Um I think you might know some of what I am going to say now? Please forgive me. This must be hard.'
Anna kept looking at Sue. She could say nothing. But she almost knew what was to come.
'My wife's name is Nancy.'
Anna gasped. Her friend at LSSPS. One of her crew.
'Oh! Nancy? How is she? We lost touch.'
God you sound stupid. She will know that.
'Nancy is well. She told me that you were a close group of friends.'
Anna nodded and smiled. For a moment she felt a nostalgic warmth. She hadn't experienced that feeling for such a long time. They had been good memories. She recalled Nancy

back then. Only her closest friends knew she was gay. Even in the late 1980s and early 90s, in enlightened London, gay women were described as – 'butch' implying masculinity. That was hardly true of Nancy with her dark hair, fashionably spiky with blond highlights, short skirts and stiletto heels. Yes, some of Nancy's friends wore jeans and boots but they were the exception. Most of them favoured the description 'lesbian' over gay, a word which Nancy had explained to Anna suited men better. Anna sighed.

'Sue please forgive me. This is a lot to take in.'

'I do know that. Bear with me though. Nancy knew what had happened to you. Then. With him. That man. She has always regretted not chasing you up. You disappeared. They all just let you go. Nancy has always felt terrible. The others too.'

'Tina. Michelle. Michael – that was his name. I had forgotten.' Anna's thoughts drifted back again to that time. They were all happy. They had worked hard. Challenged each other. They were bright. Tina, the bookish one - no make-up, spectacles and straight fair hair. But a wicked sense of fun and ability to drink most of her fellow postgrads under the table. Michelle - the sophisticated blond beauty. Not a fashionable look among students in the 1990s who wanted to appear, and often were, socially concerned and slightly eccentric. And Michael. What about him? It was hard to recall. Anna vowed to give them all some more thought when she got the chance. Sue appeared to be staring at her. Watching her thoughts almost.

'What you don't know – perhaps .....'

Anna flinched.

'That man. Simon Heath. Well he attacked Michelle. Soon after you had gone. It seems that he invited Tina, Nancy and Michelle out for a drink. He asked about you. He appeared worried. Nancy told me that he really wanted to know where you were. What had happened to you. It was if he were grilling them. As if *they* had done something wrong. Something to make you run away. But, of course, later Nancy and the others guessed something of the truth.'

Anna was mesmerized. She had believed until now that no-one had really noticed her disappearance. That they had believed her feeble excuse of illness. And they had never given her another thought.

But that has to be nonsense. Call yourself a psychologist?

'I was so upset .....' she let her voice fade. 'I couldn't imagine for a moment that anyone would miss me.'

'Nancy told me that Heath called your parents.'

'What?'

'Yes. He said so. Told them your parents had said that you were suffering from depression and didn't want to be contacted. He asked Nancy and the others to respect your wishes.'

Anna was shocked. So many times she had wondered how on earth her friends could have desert her so. She also began to connect her feelings and thoughts conceding that she had been angry with them. Then depressed and finally subsided into a morass of guilt that had prevented her from getting in touch with them.

Sue brought her back to the present.

'When we – Nancy and I heard about Heath's death we had no idea that you were involved.'

'Involved!'

'God. Sorry. I meant that there was any connection to you.'

'Sorry I get it. I know what you mean. I was involved in the appointment of a new VC. And bloody hell I was seriously upset and bloody angry that he was given priority. There was at least one woman who was better qualified. But – well that's a different story now isn't it?' and Anna almost found herself laughing.

'But you said something about knowing I didn't do it? And about him attacking Michelle? She wouldn't kill him, surely? Apologies! I'm rambling now. I think I am in shock about Nancy and the others. I'm really pleased to hear news and so disappointed in myself. Why didn't I keep in touch?'

'Nancy gets it. I expect the others do too. Would it help to meet her?'

Anna froze. The only contact she had had with any of them had been at conferences. Safe spaces where there were lots of others. No-one wanting to find out the details of her life. No-one to meddle with her mind.

'You said something about the murder. That you knew who did it?'

'No. I said I could prove it wasn't you.'

'Ok. Tell me.'

'Better if I get Nancy to tell you. Would that be too awful for you?'

Anna noticed she was wringing her hands which were getting sore.

'Where is she?'

'She's at the local police headquarters.'

'What?'

'She's a profiling expert. Criminologist.'

Anna remembered. Nancy's PhD had been about personality and aggression.

Yeh. I guess she could translate some of that into profiling.

'I'd love to see her. And talk to her.'

'She's on your side you know.'

Anna felt ashamed.

'I know'. She suddenly felt overcome with tiredness and maybe for the first time in many years she was prepared for someone to help her. Someone she trusted.

CHAPTER 28

It was strange going to see her old friend in the very police station she had spent several hours in not so long ago. Although it felt like an age had passed since the previous evening when she had been taken there – against her will she thought now. Sue suggested they walk there together. Suddenly Anna remembered that Sue was the journalist who had hounded her earlier that day.

Can I trust her? Is this all a game?

'Sue! Is all this off the record?'

'Of course. I wouldn't deceive you – and even if you don't believe that – I wouldn't deceive Nancy.'

Anna assumed that that made some sense.

'Tell me then please – do you know how Simon Heath died? All I know is that he was murdered. That it was Thursday night and his body was found at USEL. I've no idea why he was at USEL. Do you know that we were all at a reception at the King William Hotel – down the road from here? That was when I last saw him. Just before he died?'

Sue nodded. 'I understand that the event at the King William was part of the interview process.'

'Yup. That's right. We had a lavish dinner. Then I went home. I thought everyone else did too because the following day was to be the formal interview – or anointing ceremony.' Anna smiled. It had all been so exasperating but clear then. But now? Simon had left the meal and then encountered his murderer.

The two women walked on in silence both thinking about that evening. The one who had been at the dinner was trying to piece it all together. The other possibly trying to fit the facts into a story.

It was a short walk to the police station up Waterloo Bridge Road and along the south bank of the Thames, now in the shadow of the new housing blocks scattered in between small patches of grass with children's swings, small factory workshops and stretches of exhausted-looking social housing. The police station stood next to a small park and a redbrick building topped by an enormous silver extractor issuing the aroma of roasted coffee beans. Anna needed to stop herself salivating as they crossed the small forecourt containing two parked police cars. They entered the building, still dimly lit and shabby inside as Anna recalled, but she was in a very different mood from her previous visit there. When they arrived at the reception desk Sue told the clerk they were there to see Nancy Strong. Anna felt on edge with excitement in anticipation of seeing her old friend. And then there she was.

'Nancy!' She had emerged from the dusky corridor. Her hair was still dark brown, but the highlights and the spikes had been replaced by a well-cut, sleek shoulder length style that glowed even in this poorly lit interior. Her brown eyes were accentuated by black liner and mascara and the short skirts and stilettos had been changed for a tailored knee length black skirt and white blouse.

If she were anyone else, I would be scared of her!

Nancy had the air of being in control but with a kindness. *Rather maternal. I so wish I had been able to confide in her all those years ago. Maybe none of this would be happening now.*

Nancy walked up to Anna and grabbed her into a firm embrace and then turned to Sue, kissing her on the cheek.

'Come both of you. My office is on the first floor.'

Anna felt the years melt away. She also knew now that some-

one was on her side and would take over.
That would be stupid. I mustn't give in.
They entered the gloomy corridor leading from the reception area, turning left into a small lobby heading towards a staircase. They climbed, with Nancy leading the way. The first-floor corridor was bright with windows each end overlooking the Thames. Nancy's office had her name engraved on a brass plate on the door – Dr. Nancy Strong, CID.
Such a lovely name. And I know she is strong!
Nancy opened the door after shaking loose a bunch of keys that she took from her pocket. Her office, although quite small, had a sideways view of some of the new apartment blocks with glimpses of the fast-flowing river which prevented the space from feeling claustrophobic. Nancy had organized it well with a small desk in light oak against one wall mostly covered by her computer. Four ageing easy-chairs surrounded 2 coffee tables covered with papers, notes, academic journals and a few old coffee cups. Nancy flopped onto one of the chairs inviting the other two to do the same. Anna felt at home which she considered strange given she and Nancy had not spent much time with each other for many years and more so that Anna had missed her train earlier in the day to escape Sue, Nancy's wife. Even that seemed long ago now.

Anna felt so comfortable that she sat in her chair looking around the room and smiling at Nancy.
It is as if I had still been close to her even after the passing years.
Nancy too seemed relaxed smiling at her guest. Sue took the initiative.
'Ok you two. Let's get on with it.'
Nancy and Anna both laughed.
'It is so good to see you two together and please let's continue to remain friends now you've found each other. But ....'
'Yes. To business. Anna let's try to work out what is going on and what I can do to help. This is what I think has happened – but please interrupt and clarify.'

'Of course.'

'Ok then. Let's begin at the end and finish with what hap-pened while we were all postgrads. I know there is something there. Just not sure what for now. Is that Ok with you?'

Anna nodded. She felt calm for the first time since she had heard the name Simon Heath again. Despite the odd behav-iour from her colleagues at USEL, here at last someone was going to listen and help her make sense of what was hap-pening. Someone who would not blame her for whatever had happened. Nancy moved towards a whiteboard attached to the wall by the window, grabbing a marker pen from her desk. Both Sue and Anna turned slightly to face Nancy who waved her marker pen in the air before half turning towards the whiteboard once again.

'So ... well Heath – the bastard – is dead. Late on Thursday night. Yes?'

Anna and Sue nodded.

'Found at USEL. In the corridor where the VC and his staff have their offices.'

'Yes. Known as the VC's suite' Anna added.

Nancy drew a stick-figure to represent the body and Thurs-day night/USEL/VC corridor next to it.

'Found by a group of third year students who were basically out of bounds.'

'Oh! Students – the poor things.'

'Yeh – luckily for them their trespassing – trespasses perhaps I should say – were forgiven, given what they had found.'

'What the Hell was he doing there?' from Sue.

Anna nodded 'Yes. What?'

'And how did he die? Do we know he was actually murdered?'

'Christ – you don't know?'

'Well no.'

Sue and Nancy looked at each other. Anna looked from one to the other.

'What?'

'Better tell her' Sue reached over and held Anna's hand.

'His erm .. well – his genitals were cut off and he bled ...'

Anna gasped. She stared at Nancy.

'They were in his mouth – like a gangland killing. Or some kind of revenge.' Nancy paused and looked at Anna.

'I'm sorry love. I had no idea you didn't know. Didn't DI Whitaker tell you? And Henry your lawyer said nothing?'

'No.' Anna managed. 'And he must have been alive when it happened then because ....'

'I've not read the full pathologist report yet but yes, he must have been.'

'And that's why they pulled me in? because of the – Oh Christ – what he did to me? And ...' she was shaking visibly now. 'He must have done it to someone else too. Maybe more?'

'I did say ...' Sue began but stopped as Nancy met her eyes.

Nancy sat down and dropped the marker pen on the floor in front of her.

'Well you know ... Michelle? Did Sue tell you?'

Anna nodded. She was trying to mask the sobs and tears forming and spilling over down her cheeks.

Nancy picked up the marker pen and twisted it in her fingers looking thoughtful and then resolved.

'Look the three of us are going to do some thinking. Off the record. I'll get shot if anyone found out I involved you.' She looked up 'or Sue. Maybe even worse – journalist!' she looked at Sue. Anna could feel their affection for each other but also their intellectual attachment.

Anna suddenly remembered that she had students coming for tutorials from 2.30. She also noticed she was hungry – the coffee and biscuit after her lecture had become a distant memory.

'OMG Nancy – I've got to go – students. But give me a hug. I'm so bloody grateful to you Sue getting us back together. Amazing. Wonderful.'

Sue looked pleased with herself and Anna thought that she was by far the youngest of the three and quite glamorous in an intelligent kind of way. But she also recognized how Sue could be attracted to Nancy despite their age difference.

'I'll be in touch very soon Anna. In the meantime ....'

'In the meantime, I am going to try to assemble some sense about what has happened. What I now know. What I don't know and perhaps then we might get together. Where do you both live?'

'Battersea. Not too far from here. And maybe come to supper tomorrow? Bring your bloke?'

'Done. We need to catch up with what we've been doing as well as about Heath, don't we?'

And with that all three kissed and Anna went to her office.

CHAPTER 29

Two students were waiting outside Anna's office when she arrived 20 minutes later.

Jason, a mature student of Jamaican descent who had a part-time job as a mental health nursing assistant was now in his final year. He was determined to train as a clinical psychologist when he graduated. He had worked as a porter in a local psychiatric unit before being accepted to study psychology at USEL. He was unusual. Most students were younger, white and from backgrounds where their parents provided the majority of funding for their studies. Anne-Marie, leaning on the wall of the corridor was chatting to Jason. She was well within the normal range of student. Mid-length brown hair, distressed jeans over long thin legs, perfect teeth and subtle make-up. Anna was pleased with them both. They had worked hard and had made progress enough to expect upper second-class degrees and with extra effort and luck, even a first.

'Anna! Do you mind if we come in together? We're both writing the same essay.'

'Ok with you Jason?'

'Sure of course.'

'Alright then but I need to say – although I know you won't of course – that plagiarism is easily detected now – we have the software as you know.'

All 3 laughed as Anna unlocked her door.

'Sorry I am a little late. I had to meet up with a criminologist who wanted help with a case. Very interesting.' Anna muttered the last few words thinking what a hypocrite she was being.

Making excuses to students now. What bloody next?

'Please sit down ..... Oh God! What the fuck has happened?' Anne-Marie gasped, and Jason stood there with his mouth open. The room had been ransacked. The computer was on its side half the large screen was hanging over the edge of desk. Luckily its centre of gravity was firmly over the desk otherwise it would have been destroyed. The desk chair was on the other side of the office, lying on its back and the filing cabinet drawers had been wrenched open. Anna walked over to the cabinet nearest to her opening the drawer where she usually locked her handbag. It was still there but someone had rummaged through it as some of its contents were lying in the drawer while her wallet, handkerchief and a packet of tampons were lying on the floor.

Jason moved towards Anna, picked up her desk chair and helped Anna on to it.

'The office was locked. Locked.' Was all Anna managed. Anne-Marie looked pale and sat down on one of the other chairs.

Jason said: 'I'm going to fetch Sandy.' And he left the room. Anna stared at Anne-Marie who stared back looking as if she too had felt the violation of the office personally.

The memory stick!

Anna slowly turned her head towards the computer balancing on her desk. There was nothing inserted into any of the USB points. They, whoever they were, had taken it.

* * *

CHAPTER 30

J ason re-entered the room with a shaken looking Sandy.
'What has happened Anna? Are you alright?'
'Yes Sandy. Yes. But look. I need to talk to you.'
Anna turned to Anne-Marie and Jason.
'Look guys I am so sorry but we're going to have to re-arrange the tutorial.'
'Of course.' Anne-Marie answered while Jason nodded his head. They both looked concerned and still a bit shocked.
'There's nothing more you can do – I'll help Anna and she'll get back with a new appointment. I'll make sure.' Sandy smiled and the two students left the room muttering their farewells and sympathy.
'Jason, Anne-Marie – please don't say too much about this. It might frighten people.' Sandy took charge. He opened the door so the students could leave the room. He replaced the computer in position closed the filing cabinets and carefully handed Anna the items that had been thrown out of her hand-bag.
'Sandy. I was looking at the memory stick. I had locked myself in. Then someone – an important visitor. Well she asked me to go with her. To see someone. It was really necessary. Helpful. But the door was locked. Didn't anyone hear anything?'
'Hell. I don't know but I didn't. I was actually over at HR until about 15 minutes ago. So, no. I've not a bloody clue who did

this or how they got in.'

He stood up. 'I'll get you some tea. Have a look if there is anything else obviously missing. I'll be back soon'. And he left Anna to contemplate further details of the mess. A couple of framed posters had been dislodged. A rug that she had brought from her house to cover the worn office carpet had been moved and one end was curled over. The office phone had been knocked off its cradle and some files and books had been thrown on the floor.

I wonder how much of this mess is a smoke-screen? It's obvious that they came for the memory stick. But who on earth would have known about it? And who would have thought I was dumb enough to keep it inserted into my computer?

She felt a complete fool. She moved towards the chair where Sandy had placed her handbag and tried to restore the contents that had been scattered on the floor or in the filing drawer. No money or keys had been taken.

Nor any tampons! But remember that doesn't mean it was a man.

She chuckled to herself, but it felt empty. Any attempt to cheer herself up was futile.

Sandy knocked on the door as he came in bearing a mug of tea.

'How are you feeling now?'

'Tired.' Anna smiled.

'Did you get to look at the stick?'

'I did. And I made some notes.'

Sandy looked alert.

'Good. Any thoughts?'

'I couldn't hear too much but enough to find it perplexing. You know – the people who were there with each other. And who all seemed to be involved or let's say – worried about something that was ....well – shared. That's what I didn't get. People I thought had no connection other than to moan about each other or avoid any contact. That isn't the case. There they were sharing an intrigue. But ...I've not had enough head-space to think about why. At least not yet.'

'Um. I think I know what you mean but you've known them

longer. And better.'

'I guess. Yes. But then the video. Simon Heath and Shirley. So, it is true as she said they were in a relationship. But not a great one of late. As least it didn't appear so from the video.'

Sandy grinned for a moment and then looked seriously at Anna.

'But Anna what do you make of it all? Now. Who would steal it?'

'Who would know I had it?'

Sandy blushed. Anna noted it but looked quickly away to prevent his embarrassment. Then wondered why.

'I can tell you something though Sandy. I would bet quite a lot that Shirley is not the culprit. She didn't put those devices in the office. I really would bet my bottom dollar.'

'Really?'

'Why would she get involved in those encounters if she had done? She doesn't come out well and doesn't learn anything – does she?

'I guess.'

Why is he so quiet? Almost as if he has removed himself from involvement.

'Ok. Sandy, I think I must go home now. Can you report this to Security for me? I cannot take much more.'

'Of course. You go home and I'll go over there myself and get Security back here now. I have the pass key so don't worry about it.'

He went leaving Anna to wonder what on earth was happening to her life and her university.

And it all started with Simon Heath. But it's not ended with him has it?

The room was now superficially restored. No-one would imagine what had happened there that afternoon. Anna gathered her coat, bag and student papers together and sat down by her desk to catch her breath and give some thought to recent events.

Everything is changing. Seeing Nancy and feeling comfort. Re-

turning to this!

She lay back on her chair, unconsciously running a hand over her desk. An A4 sized paper fluttered to the floor.

Hey ho! Better pick it up. Don't want the cleaner to complain about the mess.

She then berated herself yet again for her gallows humour wondering why she could never take anything seriously or at least always had to include a note of self-deprecation. But then she noticed writing on the page in her hand.

Don't be late. 4p.m. under the clock at Waterloo.

❋ ❋ ❋

CHAPTER 31

Anna shuddered.

Who? Why?

She had no reason to believe that anyone would link Simon's death to her. Only a very small number of people would have been able to link the *living* Simon to her. And yet here was a prankster – or maybe much worse – teasing, provoking, taunting. She looked at her computer to see when this email trail began.

It was just last week!

Then she remembered the postcard! In the early days of last week too. That seemed so long ago. She had been mystified at first but then believed it to be from Simon. As she supposed the emails had been. She now wondered whether any of these had been from him. Although she did recall the brief encounter they had had the night he died when he implied his enthusiasm at their being reunited.

And if not Simon who? Who wants to meet me?

She was torn between a sense of terror and the need to know. She looked at the time. It was 3.40. By the time she got to the station to catch her train for home it was likely that she would pass by the clock and see who was waiting there.

Should I go now to see who is there? Should I catch the train home at Clapham Junction to make sure I don't see this person?

It was tempting to simply catch a bus to the next station on the line, but she could feel her curiosity and anger getting the better of her.

How dare he try to scare me.

Anna also considered she should call Dan and tell him she was on her way.

In that case he will know early if I go missing. Daft thought.

It also occurred to Anna that whoever she might see or even speak to at Waterloo must know something that would be of use to Nancy when they were to meet the next evening. Anna recognized now that she had informally committed herself to amateur detective work to discover Simon's killer.

And maybe the other person who was there when that happened to me.

She took a deep breath. Put her coat on picked up the bags and papers next to her chair and heaved herself up.

Ok. Here goes.

And she left her office, locked the door and set off down the corridor towards the main university entrance on her way to Waterloo.

Damn. I forgot to call Dan.

She fumbled in her bag and dialed his mobile.

'This is Dan Brosnan. Please leave a message and I'll ....' Anna hung up and dialed home. The home phone played the family message.

'Hi everyone. It's me. Just to let you know I should be with you before 6.30 – just walking to the station now. See you soon. Kisses.'

* * *

CHAPTER 32

Anna felt her stomach churning.

Her heart was racing making her feel energized and alert which she had not expected. Every sense was ready to act. She thought it rather resembled the preamble to an important presentation to fellow psychologists or to parliamentarians which she had done on a few memorable occasions. She walked across the taxi and bus lanes towards the familiar station entrance. She climbed up the steps and turned immediately to her left. As usual at this time of day people were moving in all directions – getting off trains, heading towards one of the several exits, shuffling in and out of the shops, stopping to pick up an Evening Standard, standing in groups talking or wandering slowly around in circles looking to meet someone or simply bored with waiting for a train. She had a quick look towards the clock further along the concourse but all she could see was more of this amorphous crowd.

Ok. I'm on it.

She lengthened her stride and purposefully headed towards the clock. No-one. At least there were about 30 people obviously waiting for someone but no-one she could remotely recognize. Suddenly she felt her upper arm being gripped from someone standing behind her. Gently but deliberately. She turned. For a moment she had no idea who this man was who was staring at her intently. He was blond, with dark streaks in his hair. He looked about 30, maybe more. He wore jeans, expensive trainers and a leather jacket all of which made him appear to be casually smart.

He's an academic of some kind.

'What do you want?' Anna felt less confident now.

'I called to see you in your office last week. Your secretary chap told me he'd give you a message. But you didn't show. I waited outside your room for an hour.'

Anna stared at him.

'I think I've seen you before.' She hesitated. 'Do you know Gabriel Watson?'

He smiled slowly. Nodding. 'Yes. He used to be my PhD supervisor. But I had to give it up.' He sighed. 'I found Gabriel to be such a great guy. He really put so much effort into my work. I fear I let him down. But ....' He turned away from Anna.

She felt cross and let down. Betrayed by Gabriel. But knew no reason why she thought that way.

Gabriel has no reason to link this man with me.

'I think I have seen you with him on the train.' But before he could answer Anna became angry.

'What do you want with me? Why not Gabriel? I don't know you. I doubt I can help you.'

'Look I'm really sorry. I've upset you. Made you angry.'

Anna was staring at him and beginning to retrace her steps towards the station entrance.

'Please! Humour me.'

She became even more angry.

'What the Hell do you want? Tell me or I'm going home. I'm already late.'

'Ok. Ok. Please don't go I really do need to speak to you. It's about Simon Heath.'

'Well I'm hardly surprised. You've been pretending to be him.' She glared at him. 'Haven't you?'

'I didn't know how else to grab your attention.' He looked down at his feet. She realized he was downcast and immediately felt guilty about her outburst.'

God knows why!

'Let's get away from here. Look – there's a bar on the mezzanine that is reasonably comfortable. It gets noisy so no-one will overhear us – but you are buying the drinks!'
The man looked relieved. Even happy as if he were on a date.
'What's your name? I'm guessing you know mine.' She still wanted to be spiteful and sneered slightly.
Anna led the way towards the escalator and round the mezzanine walkway to *Carole's*. Crossing the threshold between the station walkway and the bar itself was seamless, although the traditional gaggle of besuited men holding pints of beer marked the otherwise invisible entrance to the bar. They weaved their way through this throng towards a table that the man spotted. He moved quickly holding a chair back for Anna to sit. She gave him a withering look but accepted the chair gratefully loosening her coat, checking her case and handbag while maneuvering them under the table but within her awareness.
You just never know.

Anna could not forget her first time in Chicago attending a conference with a group of mature women doctoral students from USEL who had delivered a symposium. She was really proud of them and they had all gone out for a last celebratory lunch before returning to the UK. Some men at the next table, back to back with two of her colleagues were laughing, turning around to smile and laugh with her group. Chairs were shuffled and scraped and smiles were exchanged, but just before Anna and friends were served with their food the group of men left. Both groups grinning and bidding each other farewell. Nothing was amiss. Or so they believed. After the meal though Janice, one of the group, realized her handbag had disappeared. They frantically searched, confronted the restaurant staff but were eventually forced to the conclusion that they had been victims of a distraction crime. One of the men from that next table had stolen the bag.
'I'm Jim'. The man told her as he rose to buy the drinks. 'Red wine Ok?' Anna nodded. It was just what she needed she con-

fessed to herself, although not necessarily with Jim.
He returned with the bottle and two glasses. Anna was angry
with herself by then.

This whole thing is surreal. Why am I indulging him?

'There are things I need to tell you. Things you need to know.'

✻ ✻ ✻

CHAPTER 33

'**I** need to tell you who I am.'

Anna nodded staring at him, grateful that she could sip from her glass of wine.

'Years ago. When I was a kid. My mother was killed. Near Sheffield. In the Peak District. Do you know it?' Jim took a gulp of wine. She could see that his hands were shaking. Anna felt something painful stir inside. She shook her head. It was as if a piece of a puzzle was about to slip into a space that would alter her vision of life forever. And she didn't want to know what it could be. But now it was too late.

Dan.

Jim seemed unaware of her growing discomfort. Her despair. But then he placed his wine glass carefully on the table between them.

'You know, don't you? What I'm going to tell you?'

'I ... I'm not sure.' She hesitated staring at him. 'I think so. Please ... go on.'

They both grabbed their glasses and drank. They stared at each other.

'Your husband killed my mum.'

There. That was it. She knew about the woman Dan had hit with his car. His drunken friends. The tussle with the man – Jim's dad?'

But she was someone's mum.

Anna's thoughts had been with Dan when he had told her. On

his side. Anxious to square the circle. Make sense of his story so her worries about his hidden past could be eased. But now? What was this man going to tell her?

'I'm sorry. I know this is not your fault.' His eyes had welled up with tears. Anna felt she too would cry. The story was a tragedy.

'But Dan ... my husband ... it was an accident. Not his fault.' Jim's tone shifted rapidly from sadness to bitter anger.

'Well whose then? Your man was totally pissed. One of his friends tried to make things better between my dad and your husband.' He spat that word at her. Anna stared. In total shock.

'Your Dan – he punched my dad and chased my mum in his car. He deliberately ran her down.'

'No! that's not what happened. Who told you that?'

'No-one had to tell me. I was bloody well there. I saw it. I was a kid. But I saw. Those drunken doctors tried to stop that man ... your husband. Tried to stop him going for my dad. Driving at my mum. But ...' and Jim shuddered. His face fell toward the table. He placed his hands over his ears just as a child who didn't want to hear something. And then he wept. Silently. But powerfully. Anna had no idea what to do. Her instinct was to put her arms around him – to offer comfort. But this man was her enemy. He hated Dan. He doubtless hated her. And she wondered – was he right? Did Dan deliberately kill this woman?

Jim recovered himself enough to lift his head from the table, take a sparkling white handkerchief from the pocket of his jeans and wipe his eyes. He stared at Anna with his red rimmed eyes.

'You don't know do you?' He looked at her with what she thought to be pity.

What else don't I know? And what is he going to tell me now? Oh God. No. Please.

'I was in court.' His voice was quiet. Almost indecipherable now. Jim cleared his throat, mentally picked himself up

152

and looked closely at Anna's face. He noticed how puffy her eyes were. How blotchy the skin was around her cheeks and thought to himself 'She really doesn't know anything. She's unsure of him. What am I doing?' But he had to continue.

'One of your husband's – well Brosnan. He wasn't your husband then. Well one of his friends was someone powerful in Sheffield. They got him off. My mum was worthless compared with a doctor. A doctor whose friends were doctors. Whose friends had power. My dad was just a bloody worker. Worked on the railways. Not as humble as they thought. But not like them. Not a man of influence. His friends. Decent people. They comforted him. But they couldn't get my mum back. They couldn't get that man put in prison. But the court did stop him from ever being a doctor again.'

Anna continued to stare.

'Yes. That was the deal. That's what happened. He – Brosnan – he went away. I grew up. Went to university. Became a psychologist. Encouraged to do a PhD. Gabriel. My supervisor. He mentioned a Professor Brosnan. Someone I should talk to about my research.'

'Me?'

'Yes of course. You.'

'Why?'

'He respected you. I wanted to run experiments on cliques. Power. Bias. Persuasion. Gabriel said you were the expert.'

'Oh' she breathed. 'I see.'

'Then simply out of idle curiosity I looked you up. I saw a photo on the web of you and … him. Your bloody happy family. *Fuck you!*'

Anna gasped.

'I'm sorry. I didn't mean it. It isn't your fault. You didn't even know him then did you?'

Anna said nothing although she thought she might have nodded. She was torn. She wanted to comfort this bitter man but to do so would betray Dan. Her Dan. And then she wondered. Was he? Who was he?

'But why were you sending me those emails, card. All that? And what about Simon Heath?'

'Ok. That was cruel. I meant it to be. I know what he did to you.'

'What?'

'Yes. I was his research assistant at the University of Little-hampton. A two-year contract. I'd had to give up my PhD. My dad never recovered from what had happened to mum. He was weak. He had heart trouble. A stroke. More than one. We – my sister and me - got him into a nursing home in Sussex. Lit-tlehampton. There was this job. With Heath. I thought it was perfect. But what a bastard.'

'What do you mean?'

'Well he was a bully. He was sexist. Misogynist really. He groped the female researchers. Secretaries.'

Anna was horrified. 'God. That's never how he came across ....
'

'When? When you were a PhD student?'

'How do you know?'

'I know a great deal about you. I told you'

'You're stalking me.'

'No. No I'm not.' Jim sighed. He looked down at his hands on the table. He was wringing them. He looked up again glancing towards Anna's wine glass and poured them both some more. Such a simple gesture. A man and a woman having a drink at *Carole's Bar* after work. How normal it looked. It seemed. But how disturbing this meeting actually was for both of them.

'Tell me about Heath.' Anna was aware that her voice was splintering as she took a mouthful of the warming red liquid. She felt a little better.

'It was simple. He kept a detailed diary of his conquests.'

'What? What on earth ...'

'It's true. The man is vain. Arrogant. Stupid too actually. Bloody useless at research. If it hadn't been for me and some of the others - he would never had made it to professor. An-other class issue – influential family. Expensive school.'

They looked at each other and sighed. It was intimate. Almost funny. Normal. But nothing was normal. It would never be again for Anna. For either of them.

'Did you know he was going to write a book?'

She shrugged.

'His confessions.'

'You don't mean ...'

'Yeh. I do. He was going to tell the world about all the women he had had. How dumb they were. How they were begging for it and how he would give them what they wanted.'

'You're making me feel sick.'

'And I feel sick telling you. Not all men are like him.'

'I know ...' her words faded. They both realized Anna was now talking about Dan, and Jim had just been telling her something that part of her had begun to believe. She felt as if she were sinking. Going down a well. Drowning. Unable to find the strength to pull herself out. Nothing to hold on to. Anywhere. Any more.

'It's different.' Jim was trying to reassure her. It didn't work. She was sinking into despair, but she knew she had to keep listening to this man. To hear him out.

'I felt I had to warn you when Heath started bragging that he was bound to get the VC post as USEL. And no, I really am not stalking you - but I had begun to hate the thought of you. Your happiness. The pictures of you and Brosnan together. He didn't deserve happiness. He'd killed our family and got off. But I had no idea that he had married a psychologist. An academic. Why should I know? And a friend of Gabriel's?'

Anna felt a wave of exhaustion sweep over her.

Did Jim kill Heath? Was he planning to kill Dan? The kids? Me?

'There is that woman. The one here. Shirley Collins. He was seeing her until his wife found out. There was Hell to pay. You know he was so boastful. He told me and the other researchers all about it. I think we were supposed to say "Clever boy Simon. What an absolute card you are".'

They drank in silence for a while. And then Anna was struck

by a thought – what did Jim want?

'What are we doing here Jim?' she winced as soon as the words left her throat.

I sound as if I'm his bloody counsellor.

'I wanted to meet you. I wanted to make you as unhappy as I am doing. But I also … God I don't know really. I wanted you to know what Heath was really like.'

'I do.' She looked at him.

'I realize that now.'

'And now he is dead. He was murdered so you are playing a dangerous game – pretending to be him, sending me cards, emails, notes. And bloody well ransacking my office! What made you do that?'

'What do you mean?'

'You know. Of course you do. My room was turned upside down this afternoon. And I found your note to me in the wreckage.'

'I did no such thing! I would never do that. Tell me what happened?'

Anna described the scene to him and how she had discovered his reminder to meet him. She could tell as she watched him carefully that he had played no part in any of that. She experienced a mixture of relief and terror.

If not Jim, then who? Why?

❊ ❊ ❊

CHAPTER 34

Anna allowed the escalator to take her down from the bar to the platform level.

She arrived at the train in time to take a seat before the rush of late commuters forced their way onto the train. She texted Dan asking him to collect her in the car. He replied immediately. She felt a mixture of relief and dread. Why hadn't he answered her earlier phone call? Who was this man? The father of her children. The man who loved her, looked after them all. All she knew was that he would be waiting at Endlesham station which was a relief in itself as she was out of energy.

She remained in a strange semi-conscious state throughout the journey. She couldn't read. She couldn't think. She wasn't able to process the events of the long, traumatic day. She couldn't decide what was the worst thing about the day that had just passed. The journalists, the news about how Simon had been murdered, the assault on her office, the time with Jim or the news about Dan. What was so painful was that Anna believed Jim's version of the death of his mother. But on the other side of the coin was Nancy – Nancy and Sue who had given her comfort and support and had begun to help her focus some emotional strength on what Simon had done to her all those years ago.

How had Jim known about it?

'We are approaching Endlesham Station. Please ensure that you take all your possessions with you when you alight from the train.' So announced the automated train guard.

Anna could see the old Range Rover parked alongside the hedge with all the other partners and parents collecting tired passengers. She was delighted to see him – the everyday habit. But then – the terror.

Oh God. Pull yourself together. Keep strong. Solve one problem at a time. Simon first.

Anna put her mind back to this morning when Dan had been her partner, husband, best friend and the person she would trust with her life and with the lives of their children. She almost fell into his arms.

'Sorry I was out when you called earlier. I went for a swim, then it was Alison's homework and so I didn't check my phone until much later.'

Anna smiled serenely. She intended to believe him. They climbed into the car and she relaxed into the passenger seat.

'I've had a crazy day. Journalists everywhere.'

He glanced towards her.

'But – and this is exciting. One of them, Sue, is the partner – or wife – of my old university friend Nancy. Nancy and Sue have invited us to dinner in Battersea tomorrow. Can you come?'

Dan smiled. 'How lovely. Yes of course. They're gay?'

'Of course! Nancy has always been. She's a criminologist too.'

'Oh?'

'And you'll never guess – she works in the police station that I was taken to.'

'Really?' he laughed. 'And what does she know about your offence?'

'Ha ha. Seriously she does. She is involved in considering the Simon Heath murder.'

'Incredible.'

'Don't be silly – it's true. And we are going to bang out a couple of theories over drinks and dinner tomorrow.'

'Excellent.'

They were pulling into the drive now. It was quite dark and starting to rain. Anna could see the shadows of the boys in the window of the front living room and the blinking of the television.

I do hope all the homework is finished now. I couldn't take any great pressure tonight.

'So burgers for them tomorrow then – we'll be in Chelsea over Thames for a grown up evening.'

'So we shall.' Anna replied leaving the car and almost collapsing through the front door.

'And what's even better is that I shall be working from home tomorrow as I have an article to complete and no lectures! Whoopee.'

Dan looked pleased. Or so she thought.

CHAPTER 35

WEDNESDAY

Anna stared out the window.

She was still in her pyjamas and drinking tea. The days were becoming shorter and gloomier which made her pleased that she didn't have to leave the house for a few hours. She went into the boys' bedroom to chase them up. Something she hadn't had much time to do since the new term, compounded by everything that it had brought - splintering her being. The twins looked bigger now. Hairier. Taller. And she thought with all that, unlike Alison, they had become more composed. More self-reliant. Anna knew that her impression was superficial and within an hour or two they would revert to being children, but she had an image of what was to come. Two handsome young men who knew how to live well and be happy. *Something that Dan and I have accomplished together. Nothing can take that away.*

Anna considered that she was often a little hard on Alison. She wanted her to grow up faster than Alison wanted to do. But Anna was aware that reflections on her own vulnerabilities and their consequences had been damaging and she wanted to protect Alison. But despite everything Anna had a good life. She was happy, or at least she had been. Her children were happy, which was a priority, but buzzing below the surface was the ever-present worry that Alison might not be able to fight her own corner.

There was a tap on the boys' bedroom door as Alison marched in.

'What do you want?' Robert confronted her.

'I want to know where you have put my iPad.'

Anthony moved towards a small desk under the window and pulled it out from under a pile of papers.

'Thanks Ali. I needed it last night.'

Alison gave Robert a hostile look, nodded at Anthony and marched out and along the corridor holding her iPad. Anna noted that she herself had been ignored but also that Alison was far calmer than she had been in the previous academic year. This year she had begun to concentrate on the last lap of her A levels and Anna believed that her daughter might just have discovered she enjoyed her studies.

Anna sighed. There was the sound of toast popping and the smell of coffee floating up the stairs. She realized she could have breakfast without getting out of her pyjamas and the gloomy weather seemed to give her permission to be lazy. At least until tonight.

After breakfast and the quiet after the children had left for school Anna settled in her study. She was editing an article about gender and power in political parties that needed some changes before it could be published. Despite her enthusiasm for the data they had collected, along with her commitment to the research itself, this was often an irritating part of the publication process. The fine details of the article had disappeared from her memory.

So task 1: read the bloody thing again.

Task 2: try to make sense of the changes that are needed.

As she immersed herself in the subject time flowed past and before long Dan suggested lunch after which she decided it really was time to shower and dress. It was strange sitting down to lunch with Dan even though everything about the occasion was normal. Typical of how they spent their time together whenever they both worked at home. But to Anna now it was as if she were looking through a glass barrier at Dan.

Like the images you see in American prisons when they have visitors.

But who was the prisoner? And what was it that made her believe Jim, a man who had been taunting her – frightening her - with false messages? After lunch she settled back to work for a short time until the children arrived. Burgers and chips were cooking while she and Dan made arrangements to journey to Battersea for their supper with Sue and Nancy.

* * *

CHAPTER 36

Nancy opened the door looking relaxed in jeans and t-shirt and Sue emerged behind her from the long narrow hallway similarly attired. Anna noted their designer labels, but also that she wasn't envious. It was not her style. But Nancy and Sue were both so well suited to the up and coming fashionable area they had moved to which confirmed their chic image. Anna was hugged and Dan kissed on the cheek. Anna was slightly worried he would feel out of place but immediately Sue and Nancy worked successfully to make him feel welcome. They were ushered down the corridor into the living room which stretched from the front window to patio doors opening into a small courtyard garden at the back. Anna saw flower pots of all sizes some with shrubs and others with autumnal hibernating plants. Inside, the plain magnolia coloured walls were covered by paintings, many of which looked original and to Anna's eyes rather stylish. Most were colourful works showing beguiling men and women slightly out of proportion that proved particularly appealing. Several paintings involved same-sex couples holding hands or holding each other.

'This is so lovely!' she told them. They in turn looked delighted.

'We've not lived here all that long – we're trying to develop our trademark style.' Nancy laughed but it was clear to Anna how important it was to them.

'Come Dan let me get you a drink. Please sit – this is the most comfortable.' Sue had already established that Anna was to be doing the driving later so Dan happily settled into the soft leather sofa she directed him towards, with a large gin and tonic prepared by Nancy. Sue and Nancy joined him while Anna contented herself with alcohol free wine that tasted pleasant and fruity but could not compete with the gin. Even so she was relieved that she would be the most sober of the four of them as she considered she had the most to lose if the conversation should head in a dangerous direction.

No reason it should.

Nancy quizzed Dan about his background, present work, being a father of teenagers and living in the suburbs. She sounded genuinely interested. Anna reflected on Nancy's investigative skills while recalling that it was only, she, Anna, as far as she was aware who had any reason to doubt Dan.

Does Nancy know something I don't? Does Sue?

But the questioning appeared to be an act of affability and warmth and Dan responded accordingly. In fact, the evening, if this had been a normal one, was turning out to be a potential favourite. Nancy and Sue had shared the food preparation and 'supper' turned out to be an exotic culinary affair. Soup, roast chicken, home-made cheesecake, coffee, chocolates and liqueurs.

'I bet you don't eat like this every night, do you?' Dan ventured.

'Well we haven't had too many guests to practice on, but you've been the best as you really enjoy your food eh?' from Sue. Dan reached for another chocolate, dipped it into his second espresso giving a contented smile.

The group left the table at the end of the meal and moved towards the front of the living room and the comfortable leather sofas. Anna noticed that buried under a cluster of magazines, an A4 notebook covered in Nancy's writing and sketches was to be the centrepiece for the post dinner discussion.

'I'm guessing you know all about Simon Heath?' Nancy directed towards Dan. Anna was slightly shocked by this direct approach.

For God's sake how do you know I've told him anything?

But, luckily she had, and he was in the frame of mind to discuss everything lending his intellectual weight to any relevant conundrum.

'Yes. Anna has told me. And the police have been round to the house. Did you know?'

'Oh of course. So – may we all try to work out what is going on – Simon's murder and so on? And please all three of you – this is strictly off any records. Including you Sue my love.'

Sue nodded followed by Dan who agreed wholeheartedly while Anna became quietly pensive and for a while thought she might be sick. Then she rallied.

'You begin Nancy' Sue suggested. 'You have had most of the information and practice at this type of thing!' All but Anna smiled at this. Nancy looked at her.

'Please cheer up darling! I only want to help you. You know that. And you need to reclaim some of those lost years.'

Dan looked surprised at this.

'Dan sorry I think she did really well with you! I meant her work. And the upset. And losing touch with me, Michelle, Tina and Michael. We were all so close once and it was really good for us. That bastard ruined that – and that was the least of it.'

'Where shall we begin?' Sue asked. Anna recalled with a start that she had said nothing to any of them about her office being ransacked and tried to work out whether it would lead on to discussion of Jim. She thought not and decided to tell them all. Even Dan didn't know at that stage. All three expressed shock – a little exaggerated by that stage in the gin drinking cycle. Their responses reminded Anna of a pantomime, but she knew that all three were on her side.

Even if Dan has something horrible to hide it isn't to do with me. It doesn't mean he would hurt me. And I know he loves me.

'I think it may be connected to what was on the memory stick – video and sounds – you remember all of you don't you? Sandy our admin man gave them to me. The vandals have taken them.' The other three looked aghast.

'Why?' asked Nancy.

'No idea. There was nothing on them that meant much. I guess the video confirmed that Shirley Collins, my esteemed shit-faced colleague, was having an affair with Heath and she wanted him to leave his wife. She may have been blackmailing him'.

A chorus of 'yuk' came from the other three. Dan knew Shirley, and Nancy knew Simon. Sue it seemed had an empathic imagination.

'Hmm – that could suggest that Heath would try to kill her though don't you think?' Sue proposed. Dan nodded and Nancy looked at Sue enquiringly.

'Ok. Your friends Donald and John were on the audio too. Shirley and Simon on the video. Sandy had collected the spyware he knew about. What does this say so far?' Nancy wanted to bring them to order.

'Well the Donald/John chatter surprised me. They don't normally interact at all.'

'Ok. What does that mean?'

Everyone shook their heads and looked down. Nancy tried again.

'And why would Shirley have the conversation you describe with Simon if it were she who had put the camera there?'

'Maybe she thought the outcome might be different? Maybe it was more data for the blackmail? Maybe none of this had anything to do with her at all?'

'But' Anna asked 'who would want to ransack my office to find the memory stick? How did they know about it? And why does such trivia hold significance for anyone – at least now that Simon is dead.'

❋ ❋ ❋

CHAPTER 37

They drove home in a comfortable silence. Anna enjoyed driving, particularly when the traffic was light. She turned on the radio and listened to the phone-in station that kept the news up to date. Dan, who had rather over-done the gin, was happily snoring in the passenger seat with his head tilted back against the head rest. He had a small smile on his face.

He is thinking nice thoughts. Perhaps he doesn't have enough of them nowadays.

She became aware that work and parenting had gradually eclipsed their old life of seeing friends, attending and hosting dinner parties and having weekends away in Suffolk, Devon, France – the many places they had neglected for so long. She recognized that tonight had been good for both of them and that her friendship with Nancy was as alive and as beneficial as ever. And now Dan and Sue were in the mix. It was an important lesson in happiness and survival. She did acknowledge to herself, even so, that she would never have given up the parenting and the work.

After 40 minutes they pulled into their drive. Through the curtains in the front sitting room she noticed the flicker from the television suddenly disappearing.

'Dan. Wake up we're home. And do you know I think those brats of ours have been watching TV. I'm certain they turned it off just now when they heard the car.'

He stretched, sighed and laughed.

'Well more fool them if they are told off for being asleep at school tomorrow.'

She knew that she and Dan were good together and hoped that each day she could push away her memory of Jim and his story.

They entered the front door and heard the sound of retreating footsteps but then Anthony called from the landing trying to appear as if he had just come from his bedroom rather than having just escaped to it.

'Mum. Your friend Gabriel called round. About 2 hours ago.'

'Really? He doesn't usually drop in. Did he say what he wanted?'

'You of course!'

'Ha ha! You should be fast asleep and in bed' said Dan. 'You've got 5 minutes before I come up there and bounce on your head.'

Anthony laughed.

'Well he just said is "mum going to the office tomorrow?" I told him you probably were and he said he needs to talk to you. Can you be on the usual train? Yes -that's what he said.'

'Ok you guys thank you – everyone in bed now before Dad comes to chase you.'

Dan was fully awake now and laughing as he ran up the stairs to push everyone into bed. Anna moved slowly into the living room, sat on the sofa and taking out her mobile phone contemplated phoning or texting Gabriel.

What could be so urgent?

But it was really too late to call anyone. She decided she would have to wait until the morning and yes, she would catch the usual train.

But last time I did that he virtually ignored me!

She sat for a while listening to the sounds from upstairs. Some giggling, running water and thumping, as various children jumped into their beds. Anna felt she was at home. In every sense. With the children, Dan and all the amusing and irritating things they did.

But who is Dan really? Did he lie to me about something so important as the death of that woman? Jim's mother? If he did then …

✽ ✽ ✽

CHAPTER 38

THURSDAY

Back to the normal routine.

Anna always enjoyed a day working at home - all the nicer because it was a rare event. Being at home all day and every day wouldn't work for her.

It would drive me bonkers. Then I would become very depressed.

But Dan, who always worked from home, seemed to thrive on it. And yet, she thought, he is still sociable, funny and good company even with those he's only just met.

She was walking to Endlesham station mulling over her anxious deliberations. A pale sun showed itself intermittently between high white clouds. Anna wore a coat and boots now – winter wear. She wondered how Dan would spend his day, something she didn't normally give much thought to. He ran a small, a very small, publishing company and organized online book sales. The money came in. Nothing like her income. But then she was a professor in a well-considered university where research and teaching successes over recent years had provided salary hikes. Dan's interest in the publishing and bookselling business arose from his experiences in the bookshop where he and Anna had met. After their marriage they had both been content with their domestic and working lives. Maybe a bit too smug. Maybe until now. Now there seemed to be more to Dan than she ever hoped to uncover.

And as far as she knew, now there may not be a very positive discovery.

But then she recalled that she was working in the bookshop because of the trauma of being raped by Simon Heath her doctoral supervisor. She had only told Dan about this when forced to do so. When the police arrived at their home to investigate the alleged incident and then again after he was murdered.

What is the truth? What are we entitled to know about other people's lives?

Anna turned the corner arriving at the station entrance groping in her bag for her season ticket which she touched on the new contactless machine.

Today it was as if the past days had not happened. The train arrived. She saw Gabriel in his usual place. His case was on the seat next to him which she slid into as he removed it onto his lap.

'Hi Anna.'

'Hi! Are you Ok? I've been worried after last night.'

'I'm fine. But I hear you've met Jim?'

Anna looked at him and nodded.

'It was not my idea that he should meet you the way he did. I have told him I thought it was unfair to taunt you. You know. With the emails. Pretending to be Heath and so on.'

'How long have you known?'

'Yesterday afternoon – he came to see me. Told me everything.'

Anna was silent. She didn't know what to say and sat staring at her hands for almost a minute. Gabriel looked at her and grabbed her right hand in his, squeezing it.

'Why didn't you tell me? About Jim? You know what he is saying. About Dan?'

Gabriel nodded.

'You know. This is very hard. I have a lot of time for Jim. He was a great student. But he couldn't get over what happened to his mother. What he saw ..'

171

'Or thought ….'

'Look I know this is hard.'

'He was only a kid. He is likely to be wrong about who or what he saw. It was traumatic by anyone's standards.'

She paused and looked at him, removing his hand gently.

'But – well there was more to it at the time it seems. I've checked it on Google.'

'What?'

'I am – or was – only attempting to help you. And him. He's still in pain. There was something of a scandal in Sheffield over the accident at the time. But as you know I am sure the magistrate and others in powerful local positions were relatives of at least one of the young doctors. They got off.'

'Don't you think it could have been because they were not to blame? And, anyway, Dan was suspended by the General Medical Council – temporarily'

'Temporarily – are you sure?'

'Very sure – but even so he left medicine shortly after that. He was traumatized as well.'

'Ok. We should drop this for now. But what troubles me, now, is Jim's connection to Heath.'

'What do you mean?'

'Well he had opportunity …. And some degree of motive …'

'You're kidding me Gabriel. I thought he was your pal.'

'I think he had - and still has actually - so much potential as an academic. But he's fucked up. He told me about Heath's "conquest diary". And …' Gabriel hesitated. He stared out of the window. They were slowing down now at Clapham Junction.

'I know you are in it. Jim said. And I am so sorry to hear that. You must have been suffering all through the VC panels. And that bloody dinner when he tried to talk to you.'

Anna replied in a quiet choked voice 'Did you know then?'

'No. I swear. If I'd known I would have decked him.' Gabriel laughed: 'although he had a lot more potential to do that to me!'

Anna couldn't think of what to say and returned to staring at her hands. The train was pulling out of Clapham Junction. She had no memory of it stopping or the typical change-over of passengers.

'Gabriel did you know that my office was ransacked on Tuesday evening?'

Gabriel looked genuinely horrified.

'What do you mean?'

Anna told him what had happened and how that led up to her meeting with Jim. As the train reached Waterloo, she contemplated telling him about Sandy and the memory stick. But something made her pause. She recalled how she had tried to speak with Gabriel, but he had Donald in his office where they had both looked connected.

They disembarked from the train and headed for the exit. They walked in silence – companionable she thought.

But proceed with caution. I need to see Ellie. I miss her.

'Gabriel – is Ellie back yet?'

'Where's she been?'

'Well Manchester. Her mother. Her mother was ill last week - and I've hardly seen her.'

'That's strange because she and Donald were together yesterday talking about a conference paper they were writing and as far as I know she's not cancelled any classes or got anyone to take them for her. If she had gone off somewhere she would have told me for sure.'

'Or Sandy?'

'Doubtless. But she would have to see me first. She knows that. And as I said I've not noticed her absence in any sense.'

Anna suddenly felt alone. Who could she trust? Ellie?

Well at least Ellie had not been the one to tell her she was in Manchester. It was Sandy who told me. But why? He must have been mistaken but that is a little odd.

As they walked from the station to USEL they were corralled by the normal groups of students crossing the roads, taking over the walkways and pavements, walking in front of them, behind them and between them. They looked at each other and smiled. Their bread and butter. Irritating often but most were decent, enthusiastic young people whose lives were opening out.

The sky darkened slightly as one or two drops of rain began to fall. Gabriel and Anna increased their pace pushing the students, none of whom seemed to notice the weather, out of their way now. They turned into USEL, moved through the courtyard towards the Psychology Department.

'Anna come into my office for a minute would you? I think we do need to have a confidential chat.'

'Yeh - Ok. I'll just get my post.'

'No. I need to speak to you now.'

'What's just happened?'

'Come on. We won't be long.'

Anna was astounded. What did Gabriel want that couldn't have been discussed during the previous hour? She shrugged mentally and followed Gabriel down the corridor into the Head of Department's office. It was twice as big as everyone else's with an adjoining door that in the past has led into the Admin office. But since the rapid expansion of their department two other offices had been knocked through to house the administrators and Gabriel had a small seminar room and library attached to his. That room also had a door into the corridor so generally he had the adjoining door locked.

Gabriel's office was painfully tidy which set it apart from every other colleague. His long, polished oak desk, recycled from the VC suite several years ago when the top team had had an expensive refit, contained the ubiquitous computer screen, and a pile of papers in the in-tray. Sandy normally put these there before anyone else had arrived. Either side of the desk were two desk-high filing cabinets. There were four leather arm chairs of similar origin to the desk placed facing it so the occupants could see the paintings of mountain scenery on the wall behind the desk. Along the opposite wall was an easel with a flip-chart, photographs of students in undergraduate and postgraduate years and a notice board. It didn't display any outdated information. Sandy being super-efficient again Anna thought looking around the room.

He is meticulous.

Despite the formality of his office Gabriel himself was re-laxed. He rarely sat behind his desk unless he was on the computer. By the time he left for the day, papers were on the floor or scattered on the desk when he turned up the next day the office had miraculously returned to its pristine state.

Gabriel often laughed about this. Anna would have been very wary if the same had happened to her office.

'Ok. Well what I have to tell you I do with my formal HoD hat on.'

'Really? What?'

Gabriel sighed, gestured towards an armchair for Anna to sit, and took the one butting onto the front of his desk for himself. He steeled himself to look Anna in the eye.

'Look I didn't want to say anything last week – the police and all that stuff. Simon. Jim even. You know.'

'Ok?' Anna stared at him. 'What's going on Gabriel?'

'Well Donald Delaney came to see me last week.' He leaned forward and picked up a pen from his desk and twirled it between his fingers. He straightened up again.

'Well I'll come right out with it. Donald told me that you were heard making racist comments about Black students ...'

'What?' Anna almost jerked out of her chair. 'What the fuck are you talking about Gabriel? Who? Where? When? This had to be a load of bollocks.'

'He told me – err and in fact you came in while he was telling me if you'll recall – anyway that umm Shirley – yes I know what you think about her.' Gabriel hesitated. Anna was sitting very straight, eyes wide open and ablaze.

'Apparently Shirley told Donald, who then spoke to several students who said firstly that you are always making jokes about how was it that Black people had ever managed to get good enough grades to be accepted at this university ....'

'I cannot believe you are saying this Gabriel.'

He held out his hand towards her in a gesture of keeping her quiet.

'And' he sighed 'that you look at Black students – and staff – umm - Shirley in an intimidating manner which makes the students – umm and Shirley feel very uncomfortable.'

Anna stared at him. Gabriel sank back into his chair looking highly anxious after delivering his message.

'I had to report this to HR you know?'

'Why? What about evidence? You're a bloody psychologist for Christ's sake. I thought you were a friend – that you knew me. That you would know that everything you just told me is a pack of shit. Lies.

'Anna be careful about your language.'

'What are you telling me?'

'This isn't a warning. HR shall be investigating - and in the meantime they are coming here at 11 a.m. to suspend you. Walk you off the premises.'

Anna was speechless.

'On full pay of course. Until they have completed their investigation.'

'And then when they discover there is no case to answer – well then will they do something about the people who are telling these lies? Shirley? And Donald? I can't believe what he is doing or why.' Her voice trailed off. She suddenly saw red.

'I'm going home. I'll collect my mail from Admin and then you can write to me with all your formal suspension nonsense. Cancel my lectures then. Get Donald to deliver them.'

She stood up gathering her handbag and case – she hadn't even taken off her coat at that stage and walked from Gabriel's office towards the Admin base. She was in a daze. It was almost as if she had expected this.

But how could I? A bolt from the blue. Lies. A total shock.

Sandy was at his desk sifting through papers. Ellie was standing next to him looking at the same documents.

'Ellie! How are you – I'm so pleased to see you.' But Anna's en-thusiastic greeting was met with a polite smile.

'Lovely to see you too' and then with a non-committal smile Ellie turned towards Sandy saying a generalized 'see you later' and floated out of the office. Sandy looked up at Anna with a concerned frown on his face.

* * *

CHAPTER 39

'How are you?' asked Sandy.
'Fine and why are you asking?'
He looked at her continuing to frown.
'In this office I hear - so know - everything that goes on – well almost.' He looked around there was no-one else there. Sandy stood up and touched Anna's arm.
'May I walk through the quad with you? There may be things to discuss.'
Well a better offer than that offered by my erstwhile friend Ellie.
Anna nodded and they headed through the door, while Sandy steered them down the corridor and out through a fire exit.
'We don't want to meet HR do we? Come now this way.' As they left the building and across the small quadrangle at the back of the main building Anna noticed Donald Delaney at one of the windows. At least she thought so because when she looked more intently there was no-one there.
'Ok – here we are. I wouldn't normally take someone like you out where they put the dustbins but today it is our best bet for escape.'
Sandy tried to smile but there was little chance that either of them could feel light-hearted enough. Anna felt reasonably safe with Sandy but everything else she had thought she could trust and rely upon had suddenly been stripped away. Ellie, Donald, Gabriel and even Dan. She had doubts too about John, despite his 'no worries' take on professional life. She

was still shocked with what she had seen and heard via the memory stick – that John and Donald had some sort of shared cause. It made little sense given their histories. Ironically the only person she could rely upon now was Shirley – she was behaving the same way as she always did. Nasty. Mean. Duplicitous. And for very strange reasons now Shirley chose to lie outrageously to try to destroy Anna.

I had no idea she hated me quite so much.

But then Anna didn't realize how easy it would be for those she considered to be her friends, to turn their backs on her. She even wondered about Joanna in HR. Why would she believe these lies about her?

They had reached a rarely used side gate of the campus. True to Sandy's comment the gate was circled by large refuse bins. Anna needed to turn sideways to squeeze past.

'Let me go first.'

Sandy held his hand towards Anna holding her back. He moved slowly forward peering out of the gate which from the sound of it opened out into a major road – probably Waterloo Bridge Road Anna guessed. Sandy turned to her and beckoned her forward.

'It's safe. No-one around now. Good luck. Remember who you are.'

He grabbed her hand and squeezed it. At that point in time it didn't feel strange. Afterwards Anna wondered how a twenty something administrator felt able or even chose to touch her and apparently care for her in that way.

'Thanks Sandy. I shall see you again very soon. But I am grateful for your kindness.'

'Don't be!' he laughed. 'It's just how I feel right now.'

She moved quickly towards the River Thames under the railway bridges joining the different elements of Waterloo Station until she saw the South Bank complex ahead of her – the Royal Festival Hall with the bust of Nelson Mandela overlooking the steps up to the main entrance level. Anna had no particular destination in mind and was almost surprised to find herself there. But, as she was, she decided to have some tea and think. The elevator at the far side of the floor took her up to the Members' Area where she showed her pass before finding a quiet seat overlooking the Thames. She sat for several minutes watching the river flow past the forceful-looking buildings on the north bank, one of which was capped by a small clock tower and clothed with an enormous sheet. She guessed the stonework was being cleaned up.

Anna attempted to work out what had happened to her over the past couple of weeks. They had been among the most tumultuous of her life barring the time all those years ago when Heath had raped her, and through shame rather than fear, she had fled from her life. She regretted it now. Nancy had told her that she and her close friends Tina, Michelle and Michael all knew what had happened. Moreover, Michelle had been raped by him too. Anna felt guilty.

If I hadn't been such a coward he would not have attacked Michelle.

But Anna could hear Nancy's reassuring voice in her head telling her not to blame herself. Simon was the protagonist. It was his fault. She kept repeating the idea like a mantra.

Nancy. I must contact Nancy.

That decision encouraged her to get her thoughts together first.

I don't want to appear stupid. We must be partners in the investigation.

The term had started normally, bar the sudden resignation of the VC. Then she had been picked from among the rank and file professoriate to assist in appointing the new incumbent.

Someone must have thought I was worth it – at least then.

Simon and everything that that involved had come next – and then – he was dead. Mutilated it seemed. But the police had been interested in her before his murder. Someone - was it Joanna? had told the police about Simon raping her all those years ago. Anna was certain that she herself had not given permission for anyone to reveal that. She had half told

Joanna but didn't expect any action. At least not until she was sure Joanna believed her or understood the hurt and difficulties she had been through to arrive at the point she was at. Or at least the stage she had been at two weeks ago. Now everything appeared to have changed and she, Anna, was a pariah. She still could not work out why. Only Sandy seems to be on my side.

Oh God and then all that stuff from Jim. What is Joanna's role in all of this? I hadn't told her to say anything. I'd not really told her everything that had happened.

Anna left her coat and case on the table and went to the serving hatch to order a coffee and a sandwich. Despite staring at the clock over the river it took a sudden dizziness to indicate her low blood sugar. It was nearly 1p.m. and she'd not had anything to drink or eat for nearly 6 hours.

She returned to her seat and gratefully drank a few gulps of coffee. She revived slightly and even more so as she made her way through the tuna salad sandwich. She leaned back in her chair. Her brain had begun to work now. She decided not to contact Dan yet, even though she would have to tell him what had happened – but that could wait until she was home.

Nancy. I need to speak to Nancy. But only a few hours ago Dan would have been the one.

Anna knew she had to hold everything together if she were to be able to get help. She needed to distance herself from the emotional aspects of events. To be objective and maybe even to understand what was happening with her colleagues. She dialled Nancy's mobile.

CHAPTER 40

'Darling! How're things?'
'To be honest – pretty bloody. May I see you?'
'Of course – where are you?'
'At the Royal Festival Hall – shall I come to you?'
'Lunch?'
'I've had mine – but more than happy to sit and watch you.'
'Will be right there – Members' Area?'
'Yup.'

Anna moved her gaze from the river to the foyer waiting for the elevator to bring Nancy to her. It was amazing after so long. They had managed to slip into the relationship they had once had as if there had been no time between Anna's flight from her 1990s life until today. She didn't even ask herself whether she could trust Nancy – although a memory tugged a little at the back of her mind. Nancy made her feel as if she were not entirely alone in the world fighting all those dark citizens who wished her ill. 30 minutes passed. Anna continued to wait, eventually shifting her gaze from the foyer back to the river as there was no sign of Nancy coming from the elevator.

Maybe I couldn't trust her.

Anna started to tremble.

I need to get out of here fast. She knows where I am.

Suddenly Anna's phone started to shudder and buzz. It was a text. From Nancy.

Thank God.

Sudden emergency - stay where you are,
I'll come for you asap. Don't disappear on me. X

Anna's first reaction was to settle in her seat and think about another coffee. Perhaps a slice of cake. But then alarm bells began to ring once again. If she stayed where she was, she would be trapped if Nancy were to betray her. But if she left now – where would she go? Who would be there to help her?
Anna put on her coat and grabbed her bags. She headed for the elevator, descending to the lower ground floor where she could leave via a relatively little used side entrance. It occurred to her that there was nothing she had done that would suggest to Nancy or anyone else that she needed to be cornered and captured. But she experienced a strong instinct to disappear from everyone's sight. Whatever was going on, she alone would need to confront it. Or hide from it.
The basement exit was a public space where the elevator was partly obscured by a wide staircase leading to the main ground floor. She was able to observe any activity on the staircase from a side vantage-point where, if careful, she would not be noticed. Anna looked around her. No-one was using the stairs – the only people nearby were some young men and women looking at a small art exhibition on the other side of the entrance lobby. Anna guessed it was their own show.
Almost without warning Anna saw Nancy come crashing through the glass doors into the building and head for the stairway. Her hair was slightly dishevelled, and as the jacket of her dark brown trouser suit flapped against her. Anna could see a strap lying across her upper body securing a holster against her hip. Anna froze. But it was too late Nancy had seen her and rushed back down the few steps she had climbed.
'What are you doing Anna?'
Anna stared at her.

She's a cop.

'Quickly – you need to come with me. Something awful has happened. I'll tell you in the car. Come on.'

Anna, as if in a trance, followed her. Nancy grabbed Anna's arm attempting to pull her faster. The car was an official one. A young uniformed police officer was sitting at the driving seat. Nancy bundled Anna into the back seat and got in beside her.

'Please tell me what's happening?'

'I will soon. But first we need to get to the police station. You need protection.'

It was as if she were in a movie set. Fast action. Anna could not work out what was making Nancy so anxious nor why she was being taken to a police station. And why did she carry a gun? And, more so, apart from what had happened to her with Gabriel and her other colleagues, what caused this panic?

The journey from the Royal Festival Hall to the police station lasted less than 5 minutes and was only that long because of traffic. The car skidded into the access road and pulled into the car park. Nancy grabbed Anna, sliding her along the leather seat making her almost fall out of the door.

'Mo, bring Anna's bags please – up to my office.'

'Ok Dr. Strong – will do.'

Anna and Nancy moved quickly along the semi-lit corridor, the reception desk clerk nodding and waving them on. Anna was in a semi-trance. They ascended the stairs, went into Nancy's bright office where Nancy placed Anna on a chair.

'So bloody sorry to do that to you love.'

Anna stared. Trying to catch her breath she was brought back to a degree of reality by Mo delivering her handbag and case to Nancy's office.

'Anna this is Constable Jamali.'

Anna nodded 'Hi.'

'He has something to tell you.' Nancy sat down next to Anna, drew their chairs closer together and nodded to Mo Jamali. Then Nancy grasped Anna's hand. Mo sat down and arranged his chair so he could face them both. He was in his 30s Anna guessed, smooth light brown skin, short black hair and large brown eyes.

The sort you could swim in.

He cleared his throat and looked at Nancy who nodded again suggesting he begin whatever it was he needed to say.

'Professor Brosnan. I have some distressing news. An hour ago … '

He looked at the notebook in his hand. Anna hadn't noticed it before. He continued:

'.. 12.40 to be precise … I was called to the Psychology Department at USEL. It followed an emergency call – and the response fell upon me – I was in the area.'

Do I need this information?

'Please tell me what has happened. Is it Dan? My children?'

'No. No. I'm sorry – not trying to alarm you.'

'Cut to the chase now Mo.' Nancy advised although Anna noticed how Nancy herself was taking everything rather slowly.

'Ok. Dr. Ellie Hart. I believe you know her well?'

'Of course she is my …. Well I thought she was my close friend but … anyway what about her?'

'I'm sorry to tell you that she is dead.'

'Oh God.' Anna stared at him. 'What do you mean? I saw her this morning – she's fine.'

Nancy interrupted. 'Sweetheart – Ellie has been murdered.'

Anna stared from Nancy to Mo.

Mo continued. 'I'm afraid she was found in your office. I'm not going to spare you details – is that alright?'

'I think so.' Anna replied hesitatingly, looking at Nancy as if for reassurance that the details would be alright to listen to.

Mo went on: 'Her throat had been cut. Her stomach ….'

Anna's head began to swim.

'Stop a minute Mo.' Turning to Anna, Nancy squeezed her hand: 'Should he go on?'

'Yes' Anna's voice was faint.

'It's difficult to soften the blow' Mo told her. Anna nodded and tried to smile.

'She was stabbed multiple times in the stomach.'

Anna stared at him the sense of unreality kicked in once again.

'Her hands were tied behind her back. She was lying on the floor. The knife was beside the body. Her body was still warm, and her wounds were still bleeding profusely. The person who found her must have just missed interrupting the killer.'

Nancy squeezed Anna's hand once again. Mo looked at Nancy as if asking permission to continue.

What more is there? Is the worst to come?

'Her body was discovered in your office.'

'Where?' but she knew. Nothing made sense. What was the motive?

'Who found her?'

'It was her colleague Donald. He was a very close friend apparently and is heartbroken. I've not seen a man weep like that.'

Nancy gave Mo a harsh look. He blushed slightly.

'Dr Hart is about your age and height. Do you think someone mistook her for you? '

'I don't know' Anna was almost sobbing.

'What was she doing in your office?' Nancy had taken over. Anna shook her head.

'They really wanted me? Do you think that Nancy?' Anna began to shake. She then felt a wave of guilt. She should be focused on what Ellie had gone through but if they had wanted to kill *her*, she was grateful that Ellie had taken the consequences.

'Mo could you please leave us now? I'll find you later.'

Mo nodded at each woman in turn and left the room. Anna was shivering.

'This is so awful. And I don't understand. Why is this happening?'

'What do you mean?' Nancy looked surprised.

'Well like this morning – I was told I was suspended for being racist. The main accuser was Delaney.'

'No!' Nancy laughed and then checked herself.

'Ellie was very cold towards me. I hadn't seen her for several days – I was told she was with her sick mother in Manchester. But then. Well it is weird. Gabriel, the head of department, he said Ellie had been around all the time. But she must have been avoiding me. Someone is lying. But why?'

Nancy looked carefully at Anna.

'Has this to do with Simon?'

'What do you think?' Nancy asked.

'Don't you think it must? Such strange things have happened since he turned up again – and I still haven't had the chance to tell you most of it. But Ellie! I don't feel anything yet. I cannot understand.'

'Look I think the police – not Mo – he's with me – but the detectives will need to question you. That won't make it clearer. But it's best you are still perplexed – you shouldn't appear to have rehearsed.'

'Do you think it was me?'

'Don't be daft. It's me I'm worried about. You shouldn't know anything about this from me. In fact you shouldn't be here.'

Anna felt weak. What was happening? Nancy appeared as if she were about to throw Anna to the wolves. But Nancy also sounded scared for herself.

'Come on let's go downstairs and find a couple of detectives for you. Then we can talk some more.'

CHAPTER 41

Nancy guided Anna down the stairs towards the reception area.

She told the clerk that Anna had an appointment with DI Whitaker and DS Mallin.

Them again.

Anna, still stunned, stumbled around in a nightmare. One that got worse with each revelation. She remained numb which she reflected was probably the best way to be. Shortly DS Mallin arrived from the depths of the dusty corridor. He nodded politely and guided her back along it to one of the interview rooms. He beckoned to Anna to sit while he placed himself at the other side of the desk. She glanced around noting again the one-way mirror and the empty chair next to her interrogator.

'Do I need a lawyer?' she took a deep breath.

'Why?' Mallin responded. It made Anna feel guilty and a bit stupid.

Probably intended.

She retaliated. 'Well here I am being interviewed in a police station by someone who has interviewed me previously with a lawyer present. That's why.'

Mallin smiled. 'Touché! Well Dr. Strong thought I should talk to you about what appears to be a murder in your workplace. Another one that is.'

Anna looked at him and nodded.

'You don't seem surprised.'

'She told me. Briefly. I can hardly believe it – the victim – Ellie – was once my best friend.'

'Once?'

Anna sighed.

'Yes. We had been close for years. Laughed and cried at all the crap going on at work – mainly – that was it. It doesn't sound much putting it like that.'

She hesitated and looked down at her hands suddenly aware that she had been wringing them.

'But ...' she continued 'it helped us both survive all the management nonsense. And we were both very good at teaching and research.'

She pushed her hair back over her ears and scratched the back of her head.

'Do you know ... I wonder – she started being a bit cold towards me when I was chosen to be on the interview panel – the one to choose the new VC. The one where Simon ....' Anna started to recall how Donald Delaney and Ellie had made snide remarks about her being on the panel.

And it wasn't even my choice.

'I can't believe she was jealous. Surely not? But maybe she felt I was losing my principles. I really don't know. But none of this can be related to her death.' Anna began drifting into her own thoughts. She suddenly realized where she was and pulled herself into a more upright position.

'Please tell me what has happened?'

She became aware that Mallin was staring at her. He didn't appear particularly hostile. More curious.

'She was in your office.'

Anna looked at him in alarm.

What is he saying?

'She looked rather like you. Do you think .....?'

'Please don't! I know what you are thinking. It can't be. No.'

And she put her head in her hands and sobbed violently.

'She was my friend. Why would anyone want to hurt her?'

She wiped her eyes with her fist. She still shook with her sobs, before pulling herself together and faced Mallin. And then very quietly:

'You may be right. Am I in danger? I have no idea what is happening.'

The door of the interview room swept open and DI Whitaker breezed in scraping back the chair next to Mallin and briskly taking her place at the table opposite Anna. Anna believed then that she had been behind the one-way mirror for at least the last few minutes.

'Good afternoon Anna.' And then she turned to Mallin and nodded towards the recording machine. He pressed the record button and Whitaker stated the date, time reason for the recording as well as who was present.

'We have some questions for you Anna. Is there any reason that Ellie Hart should be in your office in your absence?'

'None.'

'Please try a bit harder. What do you keep there? Would it be information about students? A meeting? Something about everyday work that she needed and couldn't get hold of you?'

Anna slowly shook her head.

'How would she have gained access to your office?'

'Well the only way would have been if Sandy the administrator had let her in. Only he has the means. Even Gabriel the head of department can't get into anyone else's office without Sandy's help.'

Dorothy Whitaker turned to Mallin – they nodded to each other.'

'And each time he lets someone into someone else's office it is logged. There have been break-ins and so on.'

She took a deep breath.

I might as well tell them a bit more.

'Last Tuesday – er – just 2 days ago – my office was ransacked. I was out somewhere – lecture or meeting I can't recall right now. But it was shocking. Everything turned out – all over the place. My computer was almost knocked off the desk.

Other stuff out of drawers and filing cabinets.'

She felt sick at the memory.

'Was anything taken? From Mallin.

'No' she hesitated. Then:

'Well there was something.' And she told them the history of the memory stick particularly how Sandy had said it was based on Shirley Collins' spying devices but, how once she'd reviewed the content, it clearly it was not.

'I have notes about what I heard and saw. One thing I saw was that Shirley and Simon Heath were talking. In our admin office – before our old VC had resigned – at least as far as I know no-one knew about it. And I had no idea he would be at USEL for any reason.'

The two police inspectors were staring at her. Whitaker nodded for her to continue.

'Shirley is a professor in the department. Very unpopular. But she had been having an affair with Simon. She was upfront about it. Said he was to leave his wife for her. We were shocked. Me in particular. Given what I knew. What he did to me. And what he had done to my friend Michelle.'

'Tell me. What?'

'I learnt recently that he had raped her too. Some years ago.'

No response from the investigators. A brief pause.

'When did you last see Ellie Hart?'

'This morning. Just before …. It must have been. In the admin office. Sandy was there. She was cool towards me. But I also learned that she hadn't been to Manchester to see her mum – I had been told that. But she hadn't.'

'Who told you?'

Anna gulped. Her mind was racing. There was a common denominator through all of this. A name she kept repeating.

'Sandy.'

DI Whitaker looked at Anna's shocked face and lent forward to turn off the recording machine.

* * *

CHAPTER 42

Nancy knocked on the interview room door.

She must have been watching me too!

Anna did not know whether to feel reassured or betrayed. She chose the former – mostly because she considered she needed a friend right now and Nancy fulfilled that role brilliantly.

She kept thinking: 'Sandy! I've taken him for granted. As a friend. As a confidant. Has he been the one to disparage me? To invent things I have apparently said and done? To get me into trouble – and pretending to be my friend?'

And then: 'What if Sandy had some involvement in murder. Simon? Ellie? No! I couldn't stand that. If he did then what else?'

Anna just stared at Nancy. Her lip trembled.

'Nancy. Did you hear all that?'

She nodded.

'Can you imagine what I'm thinking now?'

She nodded once again.

'What shall we do?'

'Well sweetheart you don't have to do anything – it's *our* job.'

'But I can help. I need to know. I need to find out because if he has betrayed me in this way. Why? I've done him no harm.'

She was just about to add 'it's not fair' and recognized in time how that would sound. But she felt it even so.

Nancy turned to the police inspectors.

'I'd like to chat to Anna in my office – away from this formality. What would you guys think? Would you mind? We'll let you know of our conclusions of course.'

Anna's legs felt weak as she pushed back her chair to stand up. Mallin noticed and swiftly moved around the table to help her stand.

'Are you sure you're Ok?' and then to Nancy: 'Is she alright?'

Nancy nodded. 'I'll see she is. We'll speak later. Come on Anna – you'll be fine with me.' And Anna smiled at the two detectives and followed Nancy from the interview room, along the corridor and up the stairs. Nancy's office provided a very different environment for their deliberations.

'How do we do this then? Anna looked at Nancy who smiled indulgently.

'Well you're a psychologist – we shall brainstorm and then make a plan to take back to the detectives. I'll use the whiteboard again'.

She then wiped a few notes off the side displaying their previous efforts on Simon's murder.

'Let's go then!'

'Well firstly there was a bolt from the blue on the first morning of term' Anna was making some notes on a piece of A4 that had been drifting around on Nancy's desk.

'Well 2 bolts actually. First that our VC Adrian Hanlon was stepping down – early retirement we were told. But it was very sudden. And now, thinking about it, very strange.'

She looked up and nodded as Nancy wielded her marker pen and then wrote 'old VC goes suddenly' at the top of the whiteboard.

'Second bolt – at least for me - was learning of Simon's application for the post.'

'That must have been terrible for you – and no-one would have known would they?'

'Not at all - well I didn't think so – now I really don't know. But I messed up and fainted when I saw his application. And it got worse because then he was the favourite candidate –

there was at least one woman who had a far better CV – and then - well then it appeared he was going to get the job.'

Anna continued: 'I told the HR woman – Joanna – a decent person but then your friend – Whitaker – came to my house to question me about the "allegation". I'd not given anyone permission to talk about it. I'd not even told the whole story to Joanna although I had intended to.'

'Well. What then?'

'I had to tell Dan because of the detective. I'd never told him why I was at the bookshop in Suffolk rather than doing my PhD with you lot. He didn't know. And telling him – basically telling him that I had lied to him through our life together was almost worse than anything that had happened that week.'

Nancy sat down and scratched her head. She fiddled with the marker pen and looked at Anna.

'So apart from all the other ghastly stuff you were made – forced to make a confession. Even if you should – perhaps – should have done so before – he would not have been any the wiser if Dorothy hadn't come to discuss the rape allegation. The rape. I know that.'

'Do you? Do you believe me?'

'Yes of course – I told you about Michelle.'

Anna nodded. 'Is she Ok? We never got around to talking about gossip – probably because Dan was there - and Simon murdered ....'

'She's dead. .... Michelle.'

Anna felt her head had been hit with a hammer.

'You didn't tell me.' She could hardly get the words out of her constricted throat.

'It was about 4 years ago. She got married – to quite a nice bloke – an actor. They lived in Chichester. Did some consultancy to organizations – problem solving, leadership development – that sort of thing. Had a part-time post at the university there. Seemed happy. No kids. To be honest I didn't see a great deal of them. Then – well she was run over leaving the theatre one night. Hit and run and as far as I know nothing was ever discovered. Still an open case.'

'My God.'

'Horrendous and I'm truly sorry you didn't know. I assumed that there would have been professional announcements that everyone saw – an obituary in the Guardian actually ….' Her voice trailed off.

The stared at each other. 'Christ' Nancy said. 'Do you think there is some link here? Simon? Your Ellie? Michelle? Sandy even?'

'And if so what?' Anna desperately sifted through her memories of how any of these people were linked. Nancy leapt up holding the marker pen and rubbed some of the earlier meanderings off the whiteboard.

'Let me think. Let me think.'

'There is one thing – it escaped my memory at first, given all the other stuff, but my glorious colleague Donald Delaney was very happy about Simon's appointment. He said he was a great guy or something of the sort. An old friend even.'

'Donald bloody Delaney - I had heard he was at USEL and now he seems involved with everything that has happened to you.'

'How well do you know him?'

'Criminologist? Yeh?'

'Jesus. Of course. From what he said Simon had already conferred with him – told me and Ellie that Simon had plans to develop our department. What I also recall - and perhaps this is what had blocked my memory a bit – was that he was clearly pissed off that I was to be on the interview panel and not him. Virtually accused me of being a quisling.'

Nancy sat down again and continued to play with the marker pen. Both women sat in silence for several moments trying to make sense of everything. Eventually Nancy stood, wiped out the names from the whiteboard and listed Delaney, Hanlon, Heath and Sandy – on one side of the board and Michelle, Ellie on the other.

'Not sure what to do with Heath' so she wrote his name in brackets on the side of those who were dead. Then she added another to that list. Michael.

'You did know about him?'

Anna shivered. 'No. When? How? I'm not feeling good about this are you?'

Nancy tried to look professional and objective, but it didn't work. She sat down as tears came to her eyes.

'Michael Scott killed himself shortly after Michelle died – possibly about 3 years ago. He hanged himself. At home. He lived alone and it was a few weeks before anyone found him.'

'Oh God!'

'He had been depressed for some time. He was close to Tina and Michelle – I didn't see that much of him. But Michelle was married and living in Sussex and shortly before Michelle died Tina emigrated to Australia. A Chair in Social Psychology at the University of Western Melbourne.'

'He felt alone. But surely he had other friends? He was very popular when we were students.'

Nancy drew a deep breath.

'He saw something. Something that he couldn't forgive himself for and it became even worse later.'

'What?'

'Ok darling – I didn't want to tell you anything about this, but things are overtaking us fast aren't they?'

Anna was curious.

What is this to do with me? I'd almost forgotten Michael.

'That night. The night that happened to you ...'

Anna flinched.

'I'm sorry. Well we were all out together. You remember - Simon, Michael and us? Then it looked like you and Simon were going to get off with each other. The rest of us – at least Tina, Michelle and me – we withdrew and thought there would be more fun at another bar. And we knew there was competition for Heath's favours. But Heath drew Michael aside. Then Michael said he would go home and not come with us.'

Anna looked intently at Nancy. She was transported back to that evening – not for the first time over recent days – the feelings of guilt, terror and pain washed through her. She found herself rubbing her arms trying to clean them of the traces of that past night.

'Well I thought nothing of any of this. We were all upset when you disappeared but – well I guessed you had had enough of academic life. That you were anxious about your PhD – that sort of thing. And, of course, we had our own work and anxieties to cope with.'

Anna smiled and nodded.

'Then, as I told you. He did the same to Michelle. Michael broke down. He told me that he had been with Heath the night you were raped. He had watched. Not intentionally. He'd gone to find Simon a couple of hours after the two of you had gone to your flat. Heath had suggested that he and Michael have a drink later. Michael found the door of your flat ajar – and assuming all was well – he went in and saw what was happening. He couldn't forgive himself when Heath raped Michelle later. He thought that if he had only reported what had happened to you that Heath would be in jail and Michelle would have been safe. When Michelle was killed – well ....'

'That was all he could take?'

'Yes.'

The two women were both tearful now. Nancy offered to make tea and left the office. Anna, appalled by everything Nancy had told her, believed now it was incumbent on her to assist Nancy in any way she could although thought it needed to be secret. She stared at the list of the dead – Michelle, Michael, Simon, Ellie. The first three were linked through her and their postgraduate years. But what about Ellie? And the other side of the coin? Sandy, Donald and possibly Hanlon? Well the only thing there has to be that they have links to USEL. Sandy and Donald in the Psychology Department. Hanlon the ex-VC.

We need to find out more about him. Simon to be the replacement VC. Then brutally murdered. Ellie – with no apparent connection to anyone – pittilessly killed.

Nancy pushed her way through the door with 2 mugs of tea. Both women had wiped away their tears now and were overcome with a sense of urgency. They each had ability. This conundrum should not defeat them. After a few sips of tea they began to gather their thoughts.

'Tell me about Donald Delaney Nancy. How exactly do you know him?'

Nancy sighed.

'Well I guess the usual. You know conferences, reviewing papers he has written, research grants he has applied for. He struck me as creepy.'

'The joke in the office has always been that he resembled Donald Pleasance in Halloween!'

Nancy laughed. 'I get that. Yes. But I would say even worse. He was the proverbial friend to all but behind people's backs ..... not simple gossip – we can all do that. Vicious stuff.'

'For example?'

'Well racist. He would make sneering remarks about Black people – particularly women. About their bodies. That they were stupid. Monkey noises. Vile man.'

'I can hardly believe that – he was so huggy and smiley whenever we met. Although I always thought it strange that he would never meet outside the office – never invited us round and I tried a couple of times to get him and his wife – 3rd one – to come to dinner but there was always an excuse.'

Once more silence descended for a moment or two. Then:

'My God Nancy – what was Michael's surname?'

'Scott. Why?'

'Sandy's name is Scott.'

❋ ❋ ❋

CHAPTER 43

Raymond Mallin and Dorothy Whitaker knocked before stepping quickly into Nancy's office.

'What do you think you've found?' Dorothy said. Anna thought she looked rather impatient. Maybe she didn't like being summoned by the tame criminologist. Nancy gestured towards the two remaining chairs, perched on her desk waving her marker pen at the whiteboard.

'Let me explain'. And she did.

The two detectives took copious notes and after looking at each other Anna noticed that they had relaxed.

Maybe they don't think Nancy is quite so daft then?

'Alright. We will run a check on Sandy Scott' and turning to Anna, Mallin asked 'Is that Alexander?'

'Yes, I think so. Yes. I remember writing his promotion application. Yes. He is.'

And she wondered again why Sandy had been lying to her while she had been so supportive of him ever since he arrived in the department. She knew he wasn't too keen on Delaney. Nor did he like Shirley Collins – but Ellie? Anna couldn't believe he would hurt Ellie.

Dorothy asked: 'Can you let me have the names of others in your department who interact regularly with Ellie Hart?'

'Ok. Donald Delaney, John Jones, Shirley Collins – she is the one who had been having an affair with Simon Heath. Then Gabriel Watson – he's the head of the department'.

'And are there any other obvious overlaps with Simon Heath – other than you yourself that is?'

Anna looked sharply at her. They realized that of course she was a link to all that was happening.

But I don't think I am a suspect.

She shivered slightly.

'Well I guess I should mention Ian Fielding - he was the deputy Vice-chancellor -but after Simon Heath's death he was given the post of VC – at least in the interim. And then there is Joanna from HR. Joanna Pearce - she was the person who contacted you about the – the rape. I hadn't given her permission.' Her voice trailed off.

Anna realized that this was becoming a strain for her. She suddenly looked at her watch. It was well after 5 o'clock.

'Hell. I really need to call Dan. Let him know where I am. He must be getting fed up with this'.

She tried to laugh. 'Excuse me a minute' and she grabbed the mobile phone from her bag and stepped outside.

When she re-entered the office all three were staring at the list of names – particularly those that Nancy had added.

'Are we saying that this is the definitive list of potential witnesses?' Dorothy asked of Nancy.

Anna blurted out: 'Jim.'

'Jim?' all 3 turned to her as she moved back to her seat and sank into it. 'Yes. He kept leaving me messages. He had spoken to Sandy. Told Sandy he wanted to see me. He pretended to be Simon. And I didn't realize it wasn't Simon to begin with because I didn't know he was dead.'

Anna's voice faded slightly as she tried to recall the order of events. As far as she could, she recapped with details of all the emails, Jim's connection to Gabriel - and to Dan. Anna felt distraught thinking of Dan in connection with the death of Jim's mother and everything Jim had implied.

Well more than implied.

Anna once again began to cry. She felt she was betraying Dan. She was overwhelmed by everything. She was a lousy

mother, a lousy wife, a lousy friend and not such a good lecturer right now. She wanted to run away.

I have done that before. Run. Hidden from myself. I have to be
strong. I can't do that again.

Dorothy looked at Nancy. 'We need to take over now. Interview witnesses. Urgently now. Raymond – get everyone on
this list available for interview.'

'Ma'am.' He nodded at her.

'Anna make sure we know where you are.'

And then after they left the room to Mallin: 'we need to find
this Jim.' And with that they set off towards USEL.

✳ ✳ ✳

CHAPTER 44

Nancy moved into one of the vacant chairs once again looking intently at the information she had in front of her on the whiteboard.

'What do we think about Jim?' asked Nancy.

Try as she could Anna couldn't recall what Jim looked like - or even anything he had told her, which was strange because for hours afterward each word and each gesture he had made had been branded into her consciousness. Now it was gone. She was certain he had never given her his full name. But Gabriel would know. And, of course, she could look up everything on line – she had planned to do that anyway.

'We – or rather your police officers need to talk to Gabriel about him. He was Jim's doctoral supervisor for a time. He was like me – gave up. Went to work for Simon.'

'He even pretended to be Simon to you. Did he know Simon was dead do you think when he sent you those emails?'

'I don't know.' Anna thought she was beginning to sound like a weak cry-baby.'

Pull yourself together woman. Your life depends on this.

'I might see if I can get Mo to assist. He's not exactly normal police.'

'What is he then?'

Nancy ignored the question.

'I need to tell you officially now that we can no longer discuss the case. You are a witness. Possibly even a suspect although I doubt it. Well hope not anyway.'

Anna looked aghast.

'Sorry darling – I am just trying to protect you. And me. This is a double murder investigation and you and I – and Sue too – should not be meddling or seen to be meddling.'

'Ok.'

'And try not to discuss anything we have talked about with Dan. He may be called as a witness too – actually it is highly likely given everything you've told the inspectors about Jim and his allegations.'

'I must be going then. Back to the office. Hell I can't go there – I'm suspended! So, home. I can't think. I feel so unsettled – kind of dislocated.'

'Understandably. Maybe going home is best. I'll be in touch. In a week or two we must have a social evening again – don't you think?'

Anna nodded and smiled at Nancy as she stood up, grabbing her coat and bags as she made her way out of the office. She felt weak. Rather like a naughty schoolgirl who had just been told to go and leave the grown-ups to it. In fact, it was rather similar.

'Hang on though' Nancy said 'I'm going to see you out. Don't look so bloody miserable. This will all come out in the wash – you'll see.'

'I hope so. But I am now thinking about Ellie. I can't believe it - but I have just lost someone I considered to be a close friend. Worse – I think I lost her some time before today. Someone had turned her against me. I want to find out why.'

Nancy looked at her quizzically, smiled and accompanied her down the stairs and out into the biting dusk. They both shivered, then embraced before Anna walked along the embankment towards Waterloo station and her journey home. Somehow home felt less comforting than it had done a few days ago.

❋ ❋ ❋

CHAPTER 45

Anna arrived at the station concourse just as the train arrived, spilling out its passengers from Clapham Junction and all points west.

She quickly she managed to find an airline seat of her choice. She loosened her coat and sank into the seat leaning partly against the window secure in anticipation of a relatively peaceful journey uninterrupted by too many commuters.

What is bothering me most now? Ellie, Simon, Dan? Jim's mother? And then she remembered the other dead. Michelle. Michael. And what was so awful about those two is the way in which they were connected to that bastard Simon Heath. He had raped Michelle. Michael had seen what Simon had done to her all those years ago.

Why did he take the blame? But why hadn't he said anything? Had he been afraid of Simon? Why? And what would have changed even if he had managed to warn Michelle? How many others had Simon attacked? He would have had enemies. Many enemies.

Anna also recalled that Sandy and Michael had the same surname – but Scott was not uncommon. Could that merely be coincidence?

A large red-faced man wearing a heavy parka-type jacket plonked himself in the seat next to Anna taking up slightly more than his fair share of space. He opened his brief case, pulled out an iPad and hitched himself onto it by his earphones. Anna was pleased as he was likely to be in place for the long haul thus giving her peace to deliberate.

She decided that she needed to contact Ben Hart, Ellie's husband as soon as she could. Apart from everything else on her mind she wanted to offer her condolences. She expected him to be devastated. Fortunately – or maybe not so – there were no children. She also wanted to discover what had happened between Ellie and herself since the start of term. Anna recalled that term had barely started even though it felt like a lifetime of turmoil and distress.

She added to her mental list.

I really need to talk to Sandy. What was he trying to say to me with the memory stick and was he actually from the same Scott family as Michael?

More convoluted was the connection between Jim and Donald. Both were connected to Simon – it would seem in different ways. But even so both men knew him well – one was singularly unimpressed while the other thought Simon was a great guy. Which brought her back to Gabriel. Gabriel, Jim's former supervisor. Gabriel, Donald's boss but also someone who had been having an intense private conversation with Donald. The image of the two men in Gabriel's office and the feeling of being shut out or dismissed loomed before her.

Then she heard a pinging sound on her iPhone. A private message. Endlesham was the next stop on the line so she decided to check it after she left the train. As Anna started to shift herself into position to tighten up her coat and gather her bags she saw, and felt, her red-faced travelling companion change his position as he closed down the iPad, removing the earphones making ready to leave the train. The announcement that they were approaching Endlesham caused them both to stand and move towards the exit doors in anticipation along with several familiar faces. Anna nodded and smiled. The train stopped and the door lights indicated that passengers were able to alight.

The platform was dark despite the muted lamps along the perimeter fence. The wind was becoming sharper. Anna noticed her eyes and nose beginning to water. She crossed the bridge over the railway to the taxi rank and drop off point. She deemed herself worthy of a taxi ride home after the experiences of her day. As she moved from the nearside platform to the taxis, she saw Dan.

Oh how lovely – he must have been waiting for me!

She quickened her pace to head in his direction. He appeared to be scouring the taxi rank which was also an informal car waiting area. It was definitely him. The noise of the departing train, another arrival on the nearside platform and the light murmur of the wind, all served to reduce the chance of his hearing her call. Well she thought she would sneak up on him and pull

his hair. She smiled to herself as she moved towards him.

But then she stopped dead in her tracks. Dan had crossed the car park area heading into the ticket office.

That's strange – he must know I'm unlikely to be there?

Something made her move back towards the outer edge of the platform where the lighting was weak. She waited and watched for Dan to reappear. Nothing happened. Then she heard the train move away. Could Dan have been getting onto the train?

But where would he be going at this time of the evening? He ought to be getting the kids their tea.

The shiver that passed through her was intensified by a gust of cold wind that ripped open her unbuttoned coat.

CHAPTER 46

She paid the taxi driver.

Getting out from the car she saw the lights from her house. The front living room where the blinds had yet to be closed looked bright, cheerful and full of life. She could see the armchairs, the photos on the mantlepiece, paintings on the wall and the door to the kitchen at the back of the house. There was a light in the hallway and as she turned the key in the latch she was greeted by the smells of garlic, roasted vegetables and, she guessed, chicken. The latest news bulletin was drawing to a close on the TV in the living room and she heard multidirectional teenage voices giggling and chatting. It was a home.

'Hi Mum' the voices echoed in a chorus. Only Robert bothered to look into the hall to see her, but he returned to the others as soon as he had blown her a kiss.

'Dan?' Anna called out.

'Hi darling! you are late tonight I was getting worried. Where have you been?'

Anna, more confused than ever, moved towards the kitchen as he emerged wearing an apron and bearing a glass of white wine to hand to her. She pulled off her coat, dropping it and her bags on the floor smothering him in a bear hug.

'Hey – watch the wine!' They both laughed as she reached for the glass, took a large sip and moved with him to the kitchen where he invited her to sit, taste the sauce he was stirring, and tell him of her day. She did. She told him about Ellie's death and her own suspension. He was shocked and cross that she hadn't called him. Right then, as she related the story, both incidents sounded as if they bore equal weight. Then she felt ashamed.

'But I wonder' Dan said slowly watching her expression 'Ellie was in your office. She's your height and so on. Do you think .....?'

'Nancy asked that. I don't know. It makes me sick to think about it – either way. You know – thank God it wasn't me – then the horror of thinking an innocent person was murdered in the way she was because she was in the wrong place at the wrong time.'

'But that's the point isn't it?

'What?'

'She was in the wrong place! What was she doing in your office if you weren't there? Who did she meet there? Or who else was in your office?'

'Do you think she might have seen the door ajar and thought I was there and then ....well that's why it happened. Someone was disturbed?'

Dan looked very tired suddenly. Colour drained from his face. 'Well we need to talk to the police. I guess they'll come to see you anyway.' He recovered his energy and colouring.

'But now – the table is set. The sauce is perfect. Get everyone to take their seats – dinner is ready!' Both Anna and Dan carried the dishes to the dining table.

There was a scuffle from the living room, a series of high-pitched ringing tones as machines were turned off and a clattering as the 3 teenagers took their place at the dining table. Only the TV could be heard above the sound of spoons against crockery. Anna moved to close the front blinds and turn off the TV when she saw the news item about Ellie's murder. There were images of USEL from Waterloo Bridge Road and various staff members pushing their way through the crowd of reporters. Anna noticed faces of familiar colleagues and familiar journalists. She was almost certain that Sue Abbott was there in the background. Dan came over to join her by the TV and they both stared as, to Anna's amazement, Joanna from HR gave the official version to the BBC reporter.

'A member of our highly considered Psychology Department was found dead in the department this morning. It is unclear whether any foul play was involved. The police and ambulance services were contacted immediately and have all the relevant information. USEL is co-operating fully with all inquiries related to this case. The staff member's next of kin have been informed. That's all. Thank you.'

And with that a large man appeared from out of the shadows behind Joanna and cleared the way for her to return to the university building. The reporter then promised the viewers that they would be updated when any further news was available.

'Wow.' Dan offered.

'Let's eat' Anna managed.

'What is it Mum? I heard all that mentioned earlier – we know that's where you work. Do you know that person?' Alison asked. Anna could see all three sets of eyes upon her.

'Eat up now guys. Leave mum alone. Let her finish her dinner.'

'Exciting or what?' suggested Anthony although both he and Robert had shifted their attention slightly by that stage. 'Dad don't forget it's rugby training tomorrow.'

Dinner over, followed by staged bath and bed times, finally allowed Anna to retreat to her study. She sat on the one easy chair – a dilapidated armchair rescued from her parents' house when they downsized. She leaned back, stretched her legs out in front of her shaking her ankles to relax. She then remembered that there had been a private message on her phone that she had not seen. It was from Ben Hart, Ellie's husband. Anna went cold, took a deep breath before opening it.

Anna please come to see me. I can't bear what's happened. You were her closest friend there. Can you please message me. Please don't let me down. I need to see you. Ben X

She replied:

Ben. I'm so sorry. You're in my thoughts. When? A x

Then she was startled by the bleep indicating the immediate response:

Can you come now?

Although that was the last thing Anna had planned or wanted to do, she felt strangely comforted by the idea that Ben believed that she and Ellie had still been close. So, she agreed. It was nearly 9 o'clock and pitch dark outside. But the Harts only lived about 15 minutes away.

'Shall I come with you?' Dan asked. Anna saw that he looked tired and was probably only being protective.

'It's Ok really darling. I know Ben well enough. And he must be feeling dreadful. I do too. So it would be a chance for both of us to mourn Ellie.'

Dan looked relieved and Anna set out for the Harts' house. As she drove, Anna had enough time to wonder why he had wanted her to visit now, late at night. She hadn't thought it through before, but it did seem odd.

Perhaps he can't sleep.

She pulled into Ben's street. It was a brightly lit cul-de-sac of small detached houses built in the late 90s. All of them had short driveways although clearly several residents had more than one car which left limited opportunities for visitor parking. She managed to squeeze her car into the far end of the close, clicking the lock as she headed to Ben's house. As she got nearer, she could see that it was the only one in darkness.

How strange. I guess he is at the back of the house. He must be feeling dreadful.

She straightened up, drew a deep breath, finding her way to the front door with the help of both neighbours' outside sensor lights. As she raised her hand to knock, she heard a noise

– as if a cat had collided with a flower pot. She started and turned around. But immediately she was punched in the back and a second later, her legs were swept from under her. By design, or chance, she heard the crack and felt the pain as her head hit concrete and even more darkness fell.

❋ ❋ ❋

CHAPTER 47

The pain returned as Anna regained consciousness.
The piercing fluorescent lights of the large kitchen stabbed her eyes. She closed them quickly. She moved. Her head ached. She opened her eyes again and peered around her. She was propped up against the fridge. Someone had placed a cushion behind her. It had slipped to the floor. The world beyond the kitchen was silent and dark. Anna was scared.

Someone did this to me. They must still be here. Where's Ben?

She tried to move. Although her back felt as if someone were sticking a thousand hot needles into it, she managed to reach out towards the leg of a table and gradually haul herself into a painful standing position. She attempted to figure out why anyone would do this to her and then leave her on the floor out cold – but with a cushion? She headed slowly toward the darkened hallway bumping into a chair which made a scraping noise on the tiled floor. She stopped still. Held her breath. Listened.

Nothing. Should I call out for Ben?

She decided not. With gentle movements the pain reduced enough for her to stretch her back. She felt the back of her head – there was a lump but no sign of blood on her hand. Less and less of what was happening was making any sense to her. She felt a gripping anxiety about Ben. As she reached the hallway which was still in darkness it was deathly quiet. Suddenly she recoiled in fright. Someone was turning the key in the front door. It was too late to move. A ghostly dark figure graced the unlit entrance.

'Christ! You made me jump.' Then the voice was screaming at her. 'What on earth are you doing in my house Anna! How dare you.'

Anna was aware that her eyes were staring wide open and her mouth agape.

'Ben?'

'How bloody dare you come near me! Because of you my Ellie is dead.'

'What do you mean?'

'She hated you. Did you know? She thought you were disgusting. A vile human being. And she was right. Get out of my house. Now.'

And he grabbed hold of Anna's arm dragged her along the hallway pushing her hard out through the front door. She staggered, almost falling. The door slammed behind her and once again Anna found herself shaking violently. Eventually her brain clicked in as her thoughts started to focus on reaching her car and getting home. She managed to open the door and place her key in the ignition. Rather she concentrated on locking herself in and driving for home.

Think. Think. Focus on each step. Lock. Lights on. Engine on. Turn the car around. Drive home.

She managed. She was home. She parked in the driveway. Turned off the engine and dissolved into violent sobs.

CHAPTER 48

Dan opened the front door.

He'd seen the car lights pull into their driveway. Anna realized she must look even worse than she was feeling.

'My God Anna. Come here.' He took hold of her as she climbed out of the car. Anna considered she had a mild headache but was in control although from Dan's reaction to her arrival it seemed not so.

'What the hell has happened? Let's get you inside.' She obeyed blindly as he put his arm around her waist and virtually carried her through the hallway and into the kitchen.

'Look I'm fine. Don't worry.'

'Remember I am a doctor – at least enough of one to examine you!' He smiled at her and she responded feeling reassured.

That is strange given how I found out!

'Now sit. I'll get your coat off and have a look.'

He gently helped her remove her coat. She had a bruise down the left side of her face and her forehead was grazed. The lump on the back of her head hurt as he touched it tenderly. Gradually Anna became aware of the pain in her left arm and the back of her legs.

'Tell me. What has happened?' Dan sounded a lot more demanding than normal and Anna felt in no mood to resist. She told him what had happened and together they worked out the sequence of the attack, relating it to each of her injuries.

'It seems to me that they wanted to frighten you – very seriously but even so it could have been a hell of a lot worse.'

Anna looked at him, perplexed. She felt as if she were in safe hands. This surprised her briefly. But she no longer cared. He was looking after her and that was all that mattered.

'Ok. I think we need to go to A & E just to be sure. But I think you are alright.' He poured her a glass of water.

'Drink this now and I'll clean up the graze. Then we'll go.'

'Only water?'

'Absolutely. I cannot trust you to look after yourself, now can I?'

He left her sitting, sipping from the tumbler. Five minutes later Dan returned, cleaned the minor wound and kissed her on the unbruised side of the face.

'I've told Alison where we are going. She's still reading.'

'She should be asleep by now.'

'Working-type reading – don't worry she's fine. Let's go.'

The drive to the local hospital, that had an accident and emergency department, took less than 10 minutes as there was hardly any traffic. The waiting time was far longer because Anna was not classed as an emergency by the admissions nurse. She leaned against Dan as they sat together on the row of hard plastic seats. They were surrounded by parents and children, the latter often in silent tears or sleeping. Other patients were coughing, sneezing and snoring. One man in his fifties, whom she guessed, was worse for drink or drugs, was talking to imaginary enemies. It was a little scary but for the first time in some while Anna felt safe.

Safe enough to ask him: 'What were you doing at Endlesham station earlier this evening?'

She shocked herself with her own bluntness. Anna felt Dan's body stiffen against her and then relax as he turned to her.

'I have much to explain to you. I can't now. Not here. And, forgive me, not quite now. Please remember that I love you and our life. And I shall explain. Soon.'

And that comforted her - which she found surprising.

Anna sat in a restful silence for a time attempting to make

sense of everything that had happened – and was still happening.

Ok. Number 1. Simon. He's dead – murdered - BUT before that he was to be appointed without competition as VC at USEL. Why? And how did people accept that? Surely he wasn't killed for that reason? And then why did Hanlon resign so suddenly? Is there a connection? An innocent explanation? I don't think there can be - but I need to know more.

Second – Sandy – is he Michael's brother?

And then - Michelle is dead – murder? Is there a connection between Michelle, Michael and Sandy? Michael killing himself? Is all that my fault for not telling anyone what had happened to me? Michael's fault for the same reason? How could he have just watched what happened to me?

It was hard for her to think this through but she had to understand if she was ever to regain her life and achieve some peace.

And then thirdly – Jim – the death of his mother? Dan. Christ and what is Dan going to tell me? And can I believe him? And again – I've lost count of where I have reached but Sandy and the memory stick? Donald chatting to Shirley? And to John? And then next point - Ellie.

She trembled slightly as she thought about the woman whom she still believed had been a good friend.

Was it me they were after? And why did Ben tell me that Ellie hated me? Why? That's not how she behaved to me .... Until just before she died. And Donald. And Gabriel and even John. They avoided me. Is any of that connected?

And why the hell was I beaten up? Was it a mistake? Did those people think they were attacking Ellie? But she was already dead?

Anna's head was throbbing, and her *mind* actually hurt.

If that is possible!

Then she remembered how the police detectives had originally become involved - after she had told Joanna Pearce about what Simon had done to her all those years ago.

And I hadn't told Joanna the whole story. Nor had I given her per-

mission to tell that story to anyone. The police wanted to investigate – until they found him dead.

Anna almost missed her cue as the nurse walked up and down past the rows of seated patients calling: 'Mrs. Brosnan?' Dan, who had nodded off, jerked awake and they both made their way to where the nurse beckoned.

'Please return to your seat Mr. Brosnan. We only want to see the patient.' Dan nodded, looked at Anna encouragingly and sat down again. Anna, who had previously conducted research on domestic violence, realized that the clinicians were supposed to ensure that injured women were given the chance to report violence from a partner if that were the case and so had to be seen alone.

Anna followed the nurse. She was feeling blank. Uncertain why she was there in A & E. The short walk along the dim, rather grimy corridor reassured her.

All hospitals are like this – just like my ante-natal visits.

The nurse Anna was following stopped her brisk walk at an open door, turned and gesticulated to Anna who entered. The young doctor, blond, bespectacled and typically harassed picked up a scruffy buff-coloured file. Looked at it. He gestured for Anna to sit. He looked at Anna and put the folder back on the desk. Clearly the wrong one. He reached over to the back of his desk for another and checked her name.

'Ah I see. You've three children and lucky you – we've not seen you for several years! But now you've been beaten up. I need to ask who did this to you?'

Stupid sense of humour.

Anna looked shocked. She hesitated. Probably for too long.

'We do get cases like this'. He sat back slightly in his chair believing he was reassuring her.

'No! how can you?'

'Now please tell me what happened. We might need to call the police. I believe your husband is here?'

'Yes but the nurse wouldn't let him come with me.'

'I'm afraid that is normal in cases like this. We need the wife to feel free of intimidation. So please relax. You can tell me anything.'

'What? Do you think Dan did this? Hell no – that's nonsense. I don't know who did it.'

'Ok. Ok. I think there has been a misunderstanding, but we need to notify the police in cases of deliberate injury.'

Anna told the story as far as she could. He moved her head around, looked at the bruises and wounds, tested her reflexes and stared into her eyes with a small torch. She was prescribed codeine – 'a bit dangerous so take care'. Following which the doctor wrote vigorous notes on the file, told her to take the prescription to the hospital pharmacy and handed the folder to her.

'Please let nurse have this. Come back here if there are problems with vision, hearing or migraine-like headaches.'

Anna was also advised to take it easy.

'Take some time off work and rest. If you have non-severe headaches see your GP but other than that I think you are well enough to return home.'

Yes. I shall be having time off. Suspended.

CHAPTER 49

Dan poured them both a large whiskey.
It was after midnight by the time they reached home. Anna decided that it was time for confessions – from both of them.

'We seriously need to talk Dan.'

He added some ice to his own glass. Anna waved a hand over her own indicating she wanted to drink hers neat.

'I owe you some answers. I know that. But before I say anything please tell me that you will continue to trust me – and love me. Please?'

Anna looked into his eyes. They were both tearful which made them smile.

'You know I will. And you.'

'Of course.'

'Let's start from the beginning.'

They clicked whiskey glasses, and each took a gulp. They laughed together.

This is like evenings we spent together in the old days. Before the kids. I feel hope. Optimism. Please let that be the case.

'You start.' Anna got in first. Dan smiled and looked down into his glass which was now empty apart from the ice cubes. He stood up, moved towards the sideboard and the whiskey bottle. He poured and offered more to Anna who nodded.

'I'm not quite who or what you thought I was. You know that now don't you?'

She looked at him and nodded, gulping down more whiskey in fearful anticipation. Dan saw her terror.

'It's Ok. It's not bad I promise. But you need to hear me out …. And please this is seriously top secret.'

'I'm your wife' was all her weak voice could manage at that point.

'Well. When we met *I* knew who *you* were.'

'What? What do you mean? I'm not anyone special. I was a grad student drop-out working in a bookstore and living with my parents.'

'Special to me as it turned out. But not just at first.'

He sighed. Paused and inhaled. He was finding it hard to know how or where to begin.

'I was a doctor.'

She nodded.

'I was not disciplined, sanctioned or whatever. That's all non-sense …. '

'But ….. ' Anna began thinking about what Jim had said.

Dan held up his hand. 'Wait please. Let me explain and then you can - well challenge if you want to put it that way. I know you've been told things.'

'After I had completed my house officer jobs – around 3 years after graduating, I was recruited …' he looked at her. Then drained another glass and walked again towards the whiskey bottle.

'And for me' Anna said. And after a pause to take another sip: 'Recruited?'

'Yes. By what was then called Special Branch – like the old TV show you remember?'

She screwed up her face in a comical way.

'You're kidding?'

'No. I'm absolutely not. I had a friend – well a friend of a friend – who was a high-ranking Special Branch officer. There was suspicion of an IRA action using wide-spread poison – in London. I won't say any more and please don't ask. I was completing my Medical Doctorate – a bit like you!'

She nodded at him and smiled.

'Not quite. Whatever you lot say about your MDs - a PhD is far more work and requires better brains!'

'Mm. In your case maybe. Anyway, I was, believe it or not, doing research on antidotes for cyanide but more so nerve agents. The Russians were believed to be using them against people they suspected of betraying them – Litvinenko – about 10 years ago for example? But sometime well before that I think.'

Anna nodded.

'But what I was looking at was how to combat large scale poisoning of water, air – stuff you drink, breathe and touch.'

Anna stared not quite in disbelief. It was simply that this was not the man she thought she knew.

He had warned me! Stay strong.

'Well nothing as romantic as Russian spies – hope I didn't mislead you.' Again, a smile and another glass drained. This time he didn't refill it though.

'They recruited me to infiltrate – as a kind of expert terrorist. Don't forget my – our – name. My grandfather was from Dublin.'

'Yeh. I know but the IRA? That must have been terrifying.'

'Yes and no. It was thrilling – remember I hadn't met you. No loves. No kids. A 26-year-old part-student, part A & E doctor – and just slightly bored. Fed up with being another cog in the wheel – etc., etc.'

'Really? But medicine has such value.'

'Of course. But I was never going to make it big. Special Branch – fighting terrorists? It was amazing. *I* felt amazing. It was not difficult to be accepted – undercover I mean. These were the last days of the IRA's power I guess – a year or so before you and I met. Anyway – I managed to report on all aspects of the plan to my bosses. The culprits were arrested, and I was moved to Suffolk – out of the way until the next time. While I was there, I worked mostly on documents and in-house briefings.' He paused looking at Anna feeling concerned to identify her reactions.

'Now I need something to eat – crisps – perhaps and some cheese. You too?'

She nodded.

'You have to answer something for me now though.' And she told him all about her encounter with Jim. Dan looked alarmed.

'Why didn't you tell me this before?'

'God - I don't know – but so much has happened to me. To you. Christ you know! It was Tuesday – that's when I met him. I still don't know why he pretended to be Simon on email. And I saw you at the station – and ….' she broke into sobs at that point.

Both of them suddenly felt sober.

'I don't know who this man is.'

'Let me think. Please. Wait. I saw him talking to Gabriel on the train – more than once. I think – yes - I remember. He went to the department – spoke to Sandy – asked to see me. I couldn't – or I forgot. Something. Then I was getting these emails and texts from Simon – at least so I thought. It was before I knew that Simon was dead. But – even after. I told Nancy. Or did I? - now I can't bloody remember. Because then – well you know. Ellie. Then tonight and Ben. And heaven knows what …'

Dan frowned. 'Ok we need to be very clear now about what's going on. I'll tell you a bit – I can only say a bit – about what I'm involved with at the moment. But first let's work out who knows what.'

Anna threw her head back against the chair and stared at the ceiling. Her head was thumping, and the side of her face was beginning to feel sore. The whiskey and the painkillers were losing their effect. They hadn't pulled the curtains and Anna became aware that the sky was changing. Light was appearing through the black clouds. She looked at her watch. It was 6.30 a.m. But she wasn't tired. She was energized. There was a purpose now and she and Dan were going to work together.

We can solve all this shit. Good thing I am not going to the office...... until this is solved.

* * *

CHAPTER 50

'Jim. Who is Jim?'

Dan held onto his worried frown. 'There was never any incident near any pub I know of near Sheffield. And I made up the names and details of the friends I told you about.'

Anna continued to stare. That was hurtful. It had upset her at the time – when Dan had first told her, after she had discovered that he was not exactly the person she thought he was, some years after their marriage. When they had met, Anna had truly believed he was a gentle, unambitious bookstore manager. But then to discover he had been a doctor, disciplined and suspended and the reasons. Wow. That he had been in a car that had run down a woman and killed her. That had been a lot for her to take in. But after she had recovered from the shock and weighed up the evidence – for and against her husband - she forgave him. She then lived with the new history of the man she continued to love. And when the police arrived to question her about her being raped, Anna had had to tell him the reason she herself had chosen to work in that bookshop. She reckoned then that they were both even. That they knew each other. Fully.

But Jim. And his story. And what Dan had just told her – that none of that had been true. That was alarming in the extreme. As she realized the significance of what he had told her now, her world began to shake once again. Who was this man? Father of her children.

And I love him. I do.

She tried to think. There was much to sort out if she were ever to get her life back together. And for Dan, the children and everything she believed in she had to find out the truth. She had to clear her name too although that seemed trivial compared to what had happened to Ellie. To Michael and to Simon. And maybe Michelle?

Neither Dan nor Anna seemed able to work out who Jim might be nor why he had appeared in their life. They decided to commit all their thoughts, worries and apparent evidence to paper.

'And then maybe discuss all of this with Nancy? After all she is the expert.'

Anna agreed. So once again they focused on the mysteries that had barged into their lives.

'Ok then. Jim knew and worked with Simon. He hated him – knew he was a misogynist rapist. Found a diary of his conquests'.

She sighed and in a small voice whispered: 'including me.'

Dan grabbed her hand, squeezing and kissing it.

'Don't.'

'What did he want with you?'

'I still cannot work that out. He tried to poison me against you.' She didn't add 'and almost succeeded.'

'And why pretend to be Simon? Did he seriously believe that would make me meet him? Didn't he know I had no desire to see Simon ever again? Didn't he know Simon was already dead?'

'Maybe he didn't. His timing may have been mistaken. It's possible he wanted something else from you. Something that might set you against me, to frighten you so you might do something for him.' He paused frowning in concentration.

'What could I do? What did he need that he couldn't get from Gabriel? Gabriel has more power than me and Gabriel seemed to be his friend.'

They were both silent for a while. Was he trying to blackmail her? Was Dan telling the truth – that there was no incident with a woman near Sheffield?

But if that is true how did Jim know even to make something up about it?

She then began to think about who else may have known anything about that story. And then she remembered: Ellie!

'Dan! I remember now. I was shocked finding out about you and the woman. Running down. All that.'

'I'm so sorry please believe me – I am truly. I promise I shall never hurt you again.'

'I know but that's not what I want to say.'

'What then?'

'I told Ellie. She was such a close friend and I believed that she was fond of me …. As I was of her – I may have been wrong. Shit. I don't know now. But I told her. The whole story. There was nothing in the local paper was there? I did check. There was nothing on the internet either. I was terrified but saw nothing.'

'Well of course ….'

'I'm so sorry – but I was terrified – who *were* you? So, I confided in Ellie. She made me realize that I loved you and she believed vice versa!'

They both laughed. Sadly and quietly.

'Well. Ellie believed she knew something about my past. She wanted to support you so why tell this Jim person?'

'I guess we'll never know but she might have met him socially – or at a conference? Maybe Ellie told Gabriel. Maybe Gabriel told Jim. You know apart from you and me – us – well the story was relatively harmless.'

'Not really. Not if my friends and I had really run a poor woman over and killed her.'

'But – well if Ellie were worried about me. Being worried about you. Well she could have told Gabriel – because of concern. Nothing worse. But why he said anything to Jim …. And then why Jim should try to deceive me – so horribly ….'

'And stupidly.'

'There has to be a deeper reason. One connected to Simon. Has to be.'

Silence descended again.

'If Simon had taken up the new post of VC at USEL – what would have become of Jim?'

'Um. Well I would imagine he would have transferred along with Simon. Simon would have created a research post for him.'

'In your department?'

'Probably.'

'And Gabriel knew about Jim and his so-called mother?'

Anna looked down.

'Yes. I asked him. He said he knew. He said he had seen the evidence on Google. And he lied. And at the time I was getting over the shock – and believing this story.'

Dan looked at her.

'Sorry.' Anna said.

'No. We need to be clear. I'm no saint but I admit I am the one who had been dissembling. I had lied – or failed to tell you who I really was. I can totally understand your confusions – and that you must have been bloody terrified. Maybe you still are?'

Anna felt a great surge of admiration and warmth. She wondered whether she would have the guts to confess and then accept the other person's suspicions. *And still love them.* She recalled how Ellie had said to her that Dan, the failed doctor, was probably jealous of her success.

'He's so weak.' Ellie had told her. But it didn't seem that way now. Dan was giving her strength.

'You know Dan apart from all this – the attack on me, Ellie's murder, Simon's murder and the mystery of Jim – well I've been suspended for racist comments I would never have made. Or even thought of. I wonder where all of that came from and why.'

'You mean someone hates you? Wanted you out of the way?'

'But who could …. Someone ransacked my office. Someone

may have thought Ellie was me.' Anna started.

'Dan – Hanlon – the old VC – he's from Eire. Do you think ….?'

'What a connection with me – my work? The IRA? What was his academic subject?'

'He had a doctorate in bio-chemistry.' Anna said weakly. 'But it would have been about 20 or 30 years since he was involved in any practical research – he shot up the greasy pole as soon as he could. University of Norfolk - Dean, Littlehampton Deputy VC and then USEL about 15 years ago …'

'Oh God.'

* * *

CHAPTER 51

'Well? Did Hanlon know Simon? Were they at Little-hampton together?'

'Not sure – they may well have overlapped. But there is more likely to be an earlier connection. But not of subject. Biochemistry and criminology – not normally connected.'

'What about the greasy pole stuff? Would they have been in management together – friends? Competitors?'

'I'll check right now – see what I can find.'

And Anna reached for her MacBook, googling both their names.

'I'll get us another whiskey.' Anna chuckled as Dan moved towards a rapidly emptying bottle. Then:

'Ok. Yes - I think they did overlap – here's info about both of them from their Wikipedia profiles. When Adrian Hanlon was Deputy VC – up until about 4 years ago, Simon was head of the Psychology Department and on various research committees. He'd been there 3 years before that. So - they would clearly have known each other – even if they had no reason to be closer than familiar colleagues - they would have had reasons to often be in the same meetings.'

Dan handed her the whiskey and she took a large mouthful, scrunching up her face before smiling at him as he did the same.

'I'm just moving to the Littlehampton website to see if there is anything more – I might be able to look historically at Simon's pages.'

She took another couple of sips, frowning as she stared at the screen running her fingers over the track pad.

'I need more space – the screen is too small. Huh. OMG Dan look at this!'

'What now?'

'An old research post advertised – working with Simon. It might well be the one Jim got – but .... Christ it tells applicants to phone or email Simon.'

'Makes sense.'

'Yeh - but I can't believe this – to submit a formal application – the contact name is Joanna Pearce. Our HR woman. The one I tried to confide in. The one who has arranged my suspension.'

'Let me see.' He grabbed the MacBook.

'Jeez. Well blow us both down eh?'

Anna paused frowning and looked into her whiskey.

'She told the police about Simon – what he did to me. And ...' She stopped trying to control the flow of tears. And the heat of her rage.

The whiskey. The whiskey. Stop blubbing woman.

But it was too late. She was shaking uncontrollably while Dan gripped her in a strong embrace.

'There's a lot of evidence to sift through. And maybe we should call Nancy in.'

And suddenly Anna realized she was married to a police officer – albeit from Special Branch.

* * *

CHAPTER 52

FRIDAY

Dan and Anna sat on their living room floor each propped up against a separate armchair nursing their glass of whiskey.

Dawn had broken. Anna looked at her watch.

'It's nearly time to wake the kids.' They both laughed. The whiskey, the long night and their shared insights had made them feel giddy. Life was surreal. Suddenly there was a knock at the door. Dan leapt up heading into the hallway. He returned holding an envelope.

'Someone dropped this through the letterbox. It's for you.'

Anna reached towards the envelope looking puzzled. She tore it open.

'My God.'

'Come on what?'

'I'll read it to you.'

My dear Anna,

I had to let you know some things you couldn't have known. Forgive me for not telling you before now. If you think about me you will know I have always been on your side. And I have always appreciated your kindness, patience and that you've made my recent life bearable. But by the time you re-join your department I shall have gone – and some of your former colleagues may no longer be there either if justice is to be done.

I believe by now you have discovered that Michael your friend from long ago was my big brother. I suspect that Nancy Strong has told you what he did. How he felt after that bastard Heath did what he did to you and then to your friend Michelle. He thought it was his fault.. Michael was so lovely. Generous. Kind. But the mistake he made – being with Heath that night. Ruined his life.

For his sake and yours I wanted to make sure that it hadn't ruined yours. I don't think it has but please be careful who you put your trust in. I did try to warn you.

I didn't murder Heath - but I wanted to. I had intended to. I was as shocked as I believe you were when he 'turned up' as our potential VC. It made me sick. I can tell you that you need to think about the man you considered your friend – Donald Delaney. He had a connection to Heath. He may be the key to Ellie's death too. But, as I said, I am absenting myself – I cannot bear this any longer.

I wish you and your family all the luck and happiness you deserve.
Good bye
Your friend
Sandy.

'We need to get Nancy round here. Anna do you have her number?'

For a moment Anna stared at the letter that had fallen to the floor beside the chair she was leaning on.

'Sandy.' Was all she could say. Then she recovered. For his sake she would discover the truth.

He had tried to be my guardian angel!

She realized he did not want to be found. He was soon to be gone. As she was thinking she noticed Dan grabbing her mobile.

'Aha. Nancy Strong!' He dialled and moved into the hallway. She heard him opening the front door, closing it again and returning to the living room clearly talking to Nancy.

'Thanks Nancy. See you soon. The kids'll be out of the house by 8.30 and Anna and I'll be sitting around a strong pot of coffee.' Anna smiled nothing else to say and she moved toward the kitchen reaching for the cereal, milk, fruit and filling the kettle.

The next hour passed as if it were fast forwarded. Nothing unusual. Kids showered, dressed, fed, chasing homework, school books, school bags and out of the door. Dan followed climbed into the car with the three of them packed in. Anna was slightly worried that the alcohol must have still been coursing through his veins, but he didn't have to travel far.

No excuse. But it does give me half an hour to get myself sorted out and do some thinking.

But before she could move, Nancy's car pulled up in the driveway. Anna went to open the door and threw her arms around her friend.

'Coffee. Now. Please!'

'At your service' Anna felt relieved to be able to smile.

'You look terrible.'

'Thanks.' They both laughed and Nancy hugged Anna once again.

'So I gather there is some news – or at least some information that our mutual friend Delaney may have some connection to the Heath and the Hart murders?'

'Well – I'll get the coffee. Read this and see what you make of it.'

Anna ground some beans and set up the filter machine and returned to Nancy who was mulling over the contents of Sandy's letter lying back on the sofa.

'You know' Anna sat on the armchair opposite, 'Dan and I have been up all night and there are important things to tell you but first take a look at this.' And Anna opened her MacBook and showed Nancy the evidence of the connections between Adrian Hanlon, Simon Heath, Jim and Joana Pearce.

'And it was Joanna – who's our HR person – the one who contacted your colleagues when I had told just her about what Simon had done, and now she has suspended me for racism ....'

'Yeh - you told me yesterday - but I had forgotten - unsurprisingly given poor Ellie Hart. And the details are interesting.'

'But it was apparently Donald Delaney who reported me for being racially abusive - and our beloved colleague Shirley Collins who was, it seems, having a problematic affair with Heath - who was made to feel 'uncomfortable' about my attitude to Black people. And both told HR – that *students* of colour felt uncomfortable around me too.'

'A conspiracy against you? But why? Why not just? …. I don't know. It makes little sense to put you somehow in the centre of things that have their roots elsewhere.'

'I agree – obviously. Once again – you told me Heath was murdered by a man.'

Nancy nodded.

'Something between Heath and Hanlon must have been toxic. Hanlon had to go suddenly and without any warning – or due process – Heath was going to be shunted into his place as VC. That in itself made little sense.'

The coffee machine beeped at that point and Anna stood up heading for the kitchen. Black?'

Nancy nodded.

'Sugar?'

'One please.'

'So' Nancy said scratching her head as she sipped the strong black liquid 'USEL was left with no VC – except Ian Fielding – what about him? He seems to have gained the most from the demise of Heath and Hanlon doesn't he?'

'Not thought about that – umm - I wonder?'

'And what about you? Why did people want you out of the way?'

The front door opened and Dan entered and put his head through the door waving at the women.

'I can smell the coffee' he said as he moved towards the kitchen.

'It's time that a few formal questions were put to some of your colleagues. This next bit needs to be left with me.'

Nancy stood up, drained her cup, nodding to Dan who was

about to join them and kissing Anna on both cheeks.

'I'll keep in touch. And, in the meantime, any more thoughts – or facts. Well you know where I am.' Nancy seemed rather too light-hearted Anna thought but brushed it aside.

'So what was all that? Why rush off as I arrive?'

'Do you think that was it?'

'Not sure. Tell me what you'd been discussing.'

Anna recapped.

Dan summarized: 'it's now even more complicated then eh? Fielding enters the field so to speak.' They both laughed as they continued to drink their coffee.

It was about 2 hours later that Anna woke up at the sound of a message arriving on her iPhone. She was alone, lying on the floor, covered with a rug and next to an empty coffee cup. Dan's message said that Nancy had asked for his professional help interviewing some of the suspects. He would call her later in the afternoon.

How did Nancy know about Dan's previous life?

CHAPTER 53

Anna tried to call Dan, but he was not picking up his calls. *If what he told me is true – and why am I thinking it isn't? well then he will be interviewing.*

She decided to tidy the house, clear up the remnants of breakfast and coffee and then, when there was still no response from Dan she retreated to her study. She was late submitting a revised manuscript on bystander behaviour to a prestigious journal. It they approved the revisions to the earlier draft and publish the paper then she would receive praise from her department helping them to gain a high score in the forthcoming research excellence exercise. This was a key factor in deciding how much government money would be provided to the department for the following financial year.

All this seemed so far away from Anna's current concerns. What had been so important to her only 3 short weeks ago seemed irrelevant now. Even so working on the paper was a means of keeping her mind active and engaged in something other than amateur detective work. And if she were to be honest – fear. She had already been attacked once. Her office had been ransacked, two people she knew well – one friend and one enemy - had been brutally murdered, Sandy and Dan had deceived her about their identities.

With pure intentions? I don't know any more.

The thought made her shiver but in spite of everything Dan meant to her she knew she needed to pay attention to the worst possibilities. She had almost finished working on the changes to her paper when she heard the doorbell. She stretched, stood up slowly and stiffly realizing then just how tired she felt. The bell rang again and whoever was there had started banging impatiently on the door knocker.

She moved across the hall landing descending the stairs without thinking but then came to her senses recalling the recent dangers.

'Who is it?'

'It's Donald. Anna please open the door – I need to talk to you. Urgently.'

Her first reaction was pleasure – her friend Donald. She was always pleased to see him. For years she had felt close to him. He had been a comfort to her. They had laughed and cried together about silly things. The politics of the department. Their families.

But almost immediately this sensation of warmth and safety that had always been associated with Donald, changed to fear. Until recent events she had never understood how much he clearly hated her. Why? Envy? Did he really care that she had been chosen to serve on the VC appointment committee? How would she have felt if the situation had been reversed?

I wouldn't give a monkeys. But well I guess perhaps I might have been a little bit peeved but not enough to get him into trouble. To lie. So - what the fuck does he want?

She opened the front door. There he was. His thick spectacles intermittently disguising the expression from his eyes, his thinning light brown hair, and what she now interpreted as his obsequious smile. She had once seen this as kindly and slightly self-effacing.

Huh. The bastard. But calm. Calm don't let him know what you know.

'Donald! How lovely come in. Have some coffee.'

He gave her a half-hug – imperceptible. It made her shudder, but she squeezed his shoulder lightly in reciprocation. He walked down the hall and into the kitchen where they both sat on stools around the breakfast bar. Anna smiled, stood up and set the coffee machine with fresh coffee grounds and water.

Donald seemed slightly more awkward than usual. As if he were on edge. Anna thought they needed to talk about Ellie their apparently mutual close friend.

'Has anything been discovered about Ellie? Do you know what happened? Why?' Donald looked down at his hands that were clasped and resting on the breakfast bar. Fortunately for him the coffee machine 'pinged' and Anna stood up to organize their coffee. She didn't have to ask him how he liked it – she'd had several years of providing a coffee-making service for him in her office.

When you were my friend – at least .... So I thought.

'Thank you, Anna.' She noted that she couldn't recall when he had last used her name other than when trying to attract her attention. That was a strange formality that he was now introducing to their relationship. She looked at him and waited.

There's something not right here. I know that of course. But what?

There was a lull in their conversation filled by drinking the coffee but Anna recognized something false. She was determined not to blurt anything out – questions about Simon, her suspension, apparent racism. But she did think they might be able to discuss Ellie. She waited a little longer.

'So, Donald. It's so nice that you've come to see me ....' And she let it hang in the air between them.

'Oh. Oh yes. I have been worried about you.'

Really? I bet you are worried that you can't keep me out of the way forever.

'Nice of you Donald. But really, I am fine. Please tell me gossip. Oh - I shouldn't say that. I want to know everything about what happened to Ellie and that really isn't gossip.'

Donald drank some more coffee and looked up searching for a refill. Anna watched him, rising slowly taking his cup and pouring more. A pattern that she had enacted so many times before when he had come to her office on a friendly visit. This was something new. Almost sinister.

I need to keep my eyes open. Watch him.

'Lovely coffee. Thank you, Anna.'

Second time he's used my name in that way.

'So – well tell me what is happening. Has Ellie's murderer been caught? Do we know why this terrible thing happened? Please tell me. You said it was urgent. '

God shouldn't have said that!

'Although I'm delighted to see you of course.'

It was difficult for him to delay much longer although he tried.

'Well it seems that Ellie had been involved in …. '

'What? Tell me?' Anna became tense. This seemed bad.

'Blackmail! She had been blackmailing someone. Someone – someone academic.'

'How do you know this?'

'Shirley told me.'

'You never speak to her!' Anna retorted rapidly although wished she hadn't. She remembered the shock she had had when she had listened to Sandy's memory stick.

Well my shock is authentic. He won't know I'm suspicious of him.

'Shirley told me – no-one else speaks to her as you know. But she was really upset. It seems that Ellie had known about her relationship with Simon Heath and wanted to blurt it out – but – well …. Shirley needed support.'

'Do you mean that Shirley killed Ellie?'

Donald nearly spilled the coffee over his lap. He recovered some of his composure in time to avoid a scalding. But Anna saw that his hand was shaking as he attempted to collect himself enough to talk to her. She'd never seen him like this ever before.

'I can't believe that even she would do anything like that!' and he tried to laugh off his anxiety harking back to their former relationship when Donald, Ellie and Anna would make sarcastic comments about Shirley, defending themselves from her duplicity and bad grace.

'I think it was a man. Called Jim. You won't know him – he was a former student of Gabriel's. I met him at a conference – forensic psychology. I think – well it seems - Ellie was – how would you say – seeing him?'

'What? Surely not – she loved Ben.'

'Oh yes Ben.' Donald was stumbling.

What is going on. What's this about Jim again. Does he not know I've met him?

'I am going to tell the police.'

'About this Jim?'

'I think I should - don't you?'

'But what evidence do you have?'

'I thought you might have known about Ellie and this man. It all went on in your office didn't it?'

'What? Her murder you mean?'

'Obviously. But that's not what I was talking about. As you know.'

Anna felt strange. Angry alongside distress. The lack of sleep was getting to her as well as the dithering of Donald Delaney. Her anguish about Ellie, and everything else that had happened, was genuine and difficult to control. She resolved not to cry although she really wanted to. Later Anna reflected that her anger and distress had been useful in increasing Donald's anxiety. A thought flashed into her mind and she asked: 'Donald! You did it didn't you?'

His eyes fired up behind the spectacles. Suddenly he stood and moved to her side of the breakfast bar. She became fearful, thinking about Ellie. But before she could assess what was happening, he grabbed her arm and pulled her off the bar stool. Her cup went flying and he grabbed the neck of her t-shirt.

'You bitch. You've always hated me. You're a jealous slag. Whore-mistress.' Anna, whose face was jammed up against his, opened her mouth and stared in shock. He began shaking the rim of her t-shirt while his warm, moist breath soaked in coffee made her retch. Then he seemed to release her. She breathed in just before receiving a hefty punch to the jaw and passing out.

* * *

CHAPTER 54

She woke to the sound of a car engine.

She tried to move but her hands were tied together in front of her with nylon rope which rubbed her wrists. Her ankles were bound with a leather belt and she was lying across the floor of a small van which bumped energetically across uneven ground. Her throat was full of bile. Anna was surprised to realize that she could talk. He hadn't gagged her. What felt particularly strange was that it seemed somehow normal for Donald to have accosted and imprisoned her in this way.

Maybe I have always known he planned to do this? How many other women? Christ.

'Donald! Where are you taking me?' she felt her stomach churning. It was hard to talk.

I'm going to be sick. Focus. Focus. You'll be alright.

'Where you should be. Should have been long ago. Interfering bitch.'

Anna was quiet and tried to think. She remembered he had a weekender – a caravan near Brighton or somewhere in Sussex. She also recalled that although he often spoke of it, not one of their mutual friends had ever been invited down there. There had been some smiles and knowing winks from certain colleagues for which Anna had always rebuked them. But perhaps they knew or suspected things she did not?

Is that where he is going to take me? Why for God's sake?

'We'll be there soon.' Was all he said for the remainder of

the journey. Anna listened to every sound imagining she was playing in one of those clever detective movies where the bound and blindfolded heroine could track the journey through attending to the timing, shifting direction and passing sounds. But, in her case, to no avail.

Ha. No-one can do that in real life.

She was surprised that she was teasing herself with such thoughts when she had been assaulted and kidnapped by someone who was clearly psychopathic.

And I should know exactly what that is. No empathy. No awareness that other people have lives that don't focus on him. And this one is a bloody forensic psychologist.

Again, she reflected that she was taking this whole experience as if it were some kind of academic game. Random thoughts about the situation. But there was little else she could do. Suddenly the van slowed, turned and bumped its way slowly up an incline before drawing to a determined halt. The van shuddered as Donald applied the brake.

'Well you'll be pleased to hear that you've reached your destination.'

'*My* destination?'

'Well I shall be leaving shortly. That is after we've had a good talk.'

'Get me out of here now please Donald. You've had your game. You've frightened me. Now I want to go home. But ....
Well where are we exactly?'

'Sussex. Near Peacehaven. *Brighton Rock* – you've read it, yeah?'

Anna felt sick again.

What's he planning to do to me?

Donald got out of the van slamming the driver's side door. There was silence for about 5 minutes during which time she became increasingly terrified.

Think woman think. There's no point in panicking. You're trapped. Find a way to damage him.

She tried to move and shake off the rope shackling her hands without much luck. She tried kicking her legs with even less success.

Ok. I need to try to get my hands free. The belt on my legs isn't going to give.

She shifted herself onto her side and felt something digging into her hip.

My iPhone! God. He'd arrived while I'd been trying to call Dan.

She heard footsteps. Donald was returning. She heard him turning the handle at the back of the van. She lay still.

'Let's get you out. But don't try anything stupid. I want my neighbours to think I've brought a friend to visit.'

She looked at him. There was no pity. No fear in his eyes. He looked exactly as he did when they had been discussing grant proposals or how to present some data analysis in a research publication. Down to business, a solution in sight. But practical not emotional.

To him my predicament is no more than how to identify the results we want to show. Nothing. No feeling. No history between us. Is this how he confronted Ellie? When he killed her? I'm so sure he was the one. And now what the fuck is he planning to do to me?

Anna looked at his face attempting to catch his eye in the vain hope that some of the former humanity he had exhibited way back when they were all friends might reveal itself. But she realized it was probably too late for that now – he knew she knew he had murdered Ellie. Perhaps as Sandy suggested there was at least some connection with Simon's murder too.

Still too many loose ends for a detective. But for me – I need to get out.

Anna kept her eyes on him despite the clear knowledge that that alone would not be enough to prevent him enacting his hatred in whatever way he chose. He seemed to hold all the cards.

Except one. My phone.

He lifted her to her knees hauling her out of the van.

'Don't fall. Try to look dignified.' He hissed at her. She almost collapsed in a fit of laughter.

'Dignified hardly fits what you're doing.'

'Shut up.'

Anna looked around. The van was parked next to a small cara-van, one of about 20 others, on a grassy area surrounded by a low white fence. In one direction was a small red-brick build-ing with a door and a window. She guessed it might serve as the source of water – possibly a toilet and shower – for the small group of campers. She began to tremble as she became aware of the other end of the field. She could see a chalky edge to the grassy upward slope. But looking beyond this, towards the bay, were sheer cliffs.

He plans to throw me over. Say I was visiting and fell. I was drunk. Bastard.

Donald was leading Anna towards the small caravan where the door was already ajar. She climbed onto the stool which served as a doorstep and he pushed her inside. It was dark. He caught hold of her shoulders and steered her to the far end of the caravan forcing her down onto a bunk. Typically, there were two such berths serving as beds and seats – one each side of a small gap ready for the table to be raised in the middle. She was the furthest end from the kitchen area and shower space.

Not very far apart though. I need to get rid of him for a while. I'll tell him I'm hungry – which is true anyway.

As he had tied her hands in front of her, it made it difficult to get the rope off her wrists without being seen, even if she could physically manage it. She thought how the movies al-ways showed the prisoner shuffling her hands from behind to untie them.

Donald is brighter than those movie villains – he knows to watch me. Blast it.

'Donald. I need something to eat. Please. I'm starving. Aren't you?'

He stood at the entrance door. He looked as if he were about to leave and lock her in. He paused apparently giving her request some thought.

'Yes. You're right. I have to feed you.'

Anna thought this a strange thing to say but one that might serve her purpose.

'I need to get food.' He moved towards her, checking that her restraints were secure. Nodded with satisfaction and left the caravan. Anna heard the lock being secured from the outside. She held her breath listening intently until she could hear what sounded like the van door opening, being slammed shut and the engine revving and leaving. Progress sounded slow and bumpy just as it had been for their arrival. She waited a little longer just to ensure he wasn't fooling her - but all was silent. Late Autumn was clearly not a popular time for caravan owners to be on site. She guessed that mid-week made life even quieter in this part of Peacehaven.

Maybe that's how it got its name.

She waited for 3 long minutes before attempting to reach her phone. She lay on the bunk, hands bound on her stomach and twisted her hips. She tried desperately not to crush or drop the phone. There was at least one near miss which caused her heart to race and fingers to sweat. Suddenly she realized that part of the nylon rope was sliding up and down her wrist. There was potentially enough slack for her hands to separate slightly. Just enough to form a pincer. As she wriggled towards her right hip jean's pocket where the phone had firmly lodged itself, she was able to touch it. She felt for the smooth end – the one without the charging point and earphone hole. Concentrating hard she focused on turning it on and praying that the Family Sharing on the Find My iPhone App would kick in as it promised it would – surely Dan would try to find where she was? And they often used the same procedure for checking where the kids were.

By now Dan will be looking for me. Nancy too. Please God.

* * *

CHAPTER 55

The distant sound of a car engine reached her ears around 30 minutes later.

She lay still praying it was Dan coming to find her, wondering how long it would take Donald to find a store and buy food. She had no idea about what was available in this area. The car was drawing nearer. Once again she heard it slow down to manoeuvre the bumpy terrain. Then she almost whooped with joy – she heard another sound. A police siren.

Could it be for me? Please. Please.

She heard the caravan door being unlocked and Donald threw himself in, slamming the door behind him before drawing a large bolt across. He was breathing heavily. His face was red with effort and she could smell his stale sweat reactivated through his struggle to cope. Anna realized she had never seen him panic before. For as long as she'd known him and thought of him as a friend, he had been steady, calm, cool even when they had discussed the distastes of their job, department or university. There were numerous times when Anna had been angry at some perceived injustice in the system. Ellie had been angry about the behaviour of a colleague or student, and Anna had simply assumed Donald too had shared the emotion. But she'd never seen him like this.

Anna stared at him.

'What's happened Donald?'

'You think you're so clever, don't you? You thought that you were to be chosen as the next head of department? Well fuck you – they wouldn't want a bloody racist.'

'What the hell? Head of department? Why on earth would I want that poison chalice? What are you bloody talking about Donald?'

'You and Ellie – the good girls. The ones who were on committees. Choosing VCs. Sitting on research boards. The enhanced salaries. And why do you think she hated you? Because I told her just how you had blocked her promotion.'

Anna was dumbfounded.

Is this what it has all been about? Personal ambition? The lying bastard.

Just then they both stopped. There was a voice coming from what must have been a megaphone. She'd almost forgotten about the police in her astonishment.

'Mr. Delaney. Open the door. We want to speak to you.'

'Not bloody likely.' Donald muttered.

Then turning to Anna: 'Come here'. He grabbed her pulling her up from the bunk by the ropes around her wrist and dragged her, as she tried to hop, towards the small cubicle that housed the chemical toilet. He shoved her in, and she overbalanced landing on the lid of the loo. He pushed the door shut. Recovering from the shock she realized he couldn't lock the door from outside, but she heard him pushing something up against the door. She wracked her brain to recall whether there had been anything particularly heavy in the caravan that could hold the door closed. She couldn't remember anything being there, so she pushed gently to test. There was resistance but she also noticed a little give if she pushed hard enough. She waited heaving herself up to listen at the door.

'Mr. Delaney? Can you hear me? We know you are there. We are looking for a colleague of yours. Mrs. Brosnan. Is she there with you?'

No reply.

'We will be forced to break the door down. Please open it Mr.

Delaney.'

Anna heard nothing other than her breathing. She held her breath. And then, she could hardly believe it, but she began to smell smoke.

No Donald. You can't be doing that.

She began to kick at the door and threw herself against it. It yielded the second time. Donald was standing nearby in the kitchen area. He held a cigarette lighter. He had already set light to the curtains which fortunately appeared to be made from a heavy fireproof cotton and were simmering rather than going up in flames. Donald looked as if he were contemplating something more. He stared at her with a distracted distant look on his face. It was as if she were no longer there. Anna, unable to move very far through fear of falling over her shackled legs, felt a shot of terror rage through her.

Is he going to set us alight? He doesn't seem to be aware that I'm here.

'Donald. Open the door. I want to leave. Please. Now. Do it.'

He didn't move but at that moment the door burst open. A uniformed female police officer pushed her way in, grabbed Anna around the waist, pulling her out. They both fell down the steps and onto the stony ground. A male police officer, she guessed the one who had battered the door, pushed past them moving towards Donald. But too late. There was an explosion. The policeman fell backwards on top of Anna and the female officer, seemingly unhurt. Then the debris from the van landed on top of him as the woman police officer pulled Anna out of range before going back to help her colleague.

The explosion had not been as deadly as Anna had imagined in her panic. The male officer was Nancy's colleague Mo, whom Anna had met when he and Nancy had picked her up at the Royal Festival Hall. Nancy had told her then that he was not a run of the mill police officer. Anna had been uncertain what that had meant. She still was but she was very pleased to see him here, relatively unscathed and clearly there on a rescue mission. She wouldn't have to explain herself.

Donald had screamed after he exploded his caravan. But even he had not been too damaged by the surge of gas and flame. He was lying on the ground nursing real and imaginary wounds. As Anna looked at him, she saw the man who had been her friend – vulnerable and familiar. But as Mo and Mary, his colleague, cut the ropes that bound her wrists and feet, she could also see a nasty, even an evil, man who wished her harm and had probably murdered her friend Ellie merely because he envied her status at the university.

Mo handcuffed Donald, speaking on his radio as he led him to the police car. Mary checked Anna was unhurt and smiled at her. For Anna once again the rescue experience felt surreal. It was as if it had all been over in seconds but at some time during the drama, the sun had set, and it was now dark. Anna looked at her watch – 7.30. She wished she was home with Dan and the children.

Her iPhone rang. It was Nancy. Before too long Nancy and Dan arrived to take her home. They drove away from the collapsed caravan, following the car holding the prisoner Donald, as a local police car arrived to secure the scene of the crime.

Was there a crime? Why hell yes – he kidnapped and hit me. Why does this feel so bloody strange?

❋ ❋ ❋

CHAPTER 56

Nancy and Dan between them helped Anna into Nancy's car.

Anna's legs and arms still felt as if they were bound and her back and hips felt stiff. As if I were an old woman. 'Do you realize how long you were tied up?' Nancy asked. 'No wonder you feel stiff and sore. But you'll get over it. I think your nightmare is coming to an end.'

'It has peaked you mean? Reached a crescendo?'

Dan, who was in the back seat behind Anna, kept stroking her neck. He hadn't said a great deal. Anna concluded that he may well have been suffering from shock. Perhaps he had been more traumatized by her disappearance than she had herself? For Anna it had all been surreal. For Dan there would have been the terror of helplessness in the face of an unknown threat.

'I think I know somewhere we can stop and get supper' Nancy volunteered. Anna touched her arm: 'Oh yes please. That bastard was supposed to be getting me some food. I've not eaten since breakfast.'

'Provided we don't lose momentum for sorting out Delaney then it's yes from me too' Dan agreed.

Ten minutes later they pulled into a pub car park somewhere north of the Sussex Downs.

'Christ I really need to pee' and Anna marched ahead of the other two to seek the Ladies toilet. Nancy and Dan found a table after ordering chicken and chips and coke for 3.'

As she headed back into the main bar, she was stunned to see Nancy and Dan sitting with their heads close together engaged in what appeared to be an intense, intimate, conversation.

It's as if they knew each other. But they've only met once before.

As she approached Nancy looked up, smiling holding out her hand towards Anna, guiding her to the seat between her and Dan.

'What's going on?' Anna felt tense once again.

I know they're not sleeping together – but what then?

Dan exhaled. It was as if he had held his breath forever. He moved closer and grabbed her hand. Anna started, sat up and looked closely at his face. She was aware of Nancy relaxing back into her own chair giving Dan the front of stage.

'I am so sorry' Dan began.

Not a good start.

'I'm fed up with being apologized to – as if I were a child.'

'That's my girl' from Nancy. Dan gave her a sharp look then both of them laughed. It didn't improve Anna's demeanour, but she became aware that for the first time for a couple of weeks she was angry.

Not scared. Not apologetic. Not fainting or shaking. Just bloody furious.

She gradually began to feel able to cope with whatever shock these two were going to give her. She nodded towards Dan.

'You'd better go on then.'

'Ok. I'll start. Do you remember when we talked about me - Special Branch and the bookshop that I told you that I *did* know who you were. Even then?'

'Mmm. Yes, I had forgotten but yes, it stayed with me for a while. But at the time there had been so much to take in .....'

'I know. And I'm not going to apologize again. But this involves both Nancy and me. Hey - don't look so cross!' he said in response to Anna shifting position and shaking off his hand. Nancy reached over to Anna but she shook Nancy away too.

'Let me' to Dan from Nancy.

'Look love. Do you remember what my thesis was about? I was researching undercover policing. I had to sign what was then called the Official Secrets Act – so I couldn't even tell my friends exactly what I was doing.'

She laughed and so did Dan which irritated Anna. Even so she wanted Nancy to continue. She realized she was eventually to find something out.

'So – well. Well …. I met Dan. I *interviewed* Dan.' Anna looked at him sharply. He looked down at his hands and then nodded to Nancy to continue. Just as she was about to say more the waitress arrived with 3 plates of chicken and chips. And the coke. They all looked relieved. All 3 immediately attacked their meals. There was a sense of relief and a chance for some reflection before Anna asked Nancy to go on.

'Of course, neither of you had met and I didn't give that possibility for the future any thought. Why on earth should I? But then – after what happened to you and you disappeared - and then Heath told us that your parents told him that you wanted to be left in peace ….'

'Bloody liar' Anna and Dan spoke in unison.

'Well then I went to see Dan again to interview him about pulling out from his undercover work with ….can I say?'

'Yes, she knows about the IRA.'

'Well he happened to tell me about this woman – you – and you doing a PhD and all that. And all I told him was that we had been friends but you had wanted to be left alone. And we had no more to do with any of this until you came to our house.'

'Really?'

'Of course.' And Dan nodded vigorously.

'It was only when we met again and I heard your surname that I expected to meet Dan again. Naturally he would fall for you.'

Anna felt relief – she had had some moments of tension about

Nancy. But also felt a little irritated and patronized. *I need to let that pass. Grow up woman.*

'I couldn't say anything to you then. Shouldn't even now. I'm not going to say sorry again as I know it makes you cross. But please forgive me.' Anna smiled and grabbed both of their hands, then let them go and all of a sudden recovered her appetite.

❋ ❋ ❋

CHAPTER 57

SATURDAY

They reached London around midnight Friday.

'Delaney will be at the police station - under lock and key thank goodness. But I think we all ought to get some sleep. I'll call you both in the morning because Dorothy will need to speak to you at length Anna. And in the meantime, I think Mo has uncovered some interesting things that you might want to know about too – but not yet. I have to follow protocol and speak with Dorothy.'

On one level Anna felt frustrated – she wanted everything resolved as soon as possible. She was also curious.

There are things I am going to discover – probably things I could never have guessed.

Even so, she knew what Nancy was telling them made sense. There was little choice anyway – they were dealing with the police. Dan had left the family car at Nancy's house. They collected it, declining Nancy's offer of a nightcap. It only took less than 30 minutes to drive home.

'Alison has been babysitting by the way. She's feeling appreciated that she was left in charge. Very grown up and I think she intended to be patient with the boys for once in their lives.'

Anna gasped. 'I've hardly given them a thought since trying to get any one of you to find my phone! What a shit mother.'

They grinned at each other. Anna felt more relaxed than she

had done ever since the start of term. Life was back to normal although so much about her life had changed as well. She sighed. They both went to bed and neither woke up until Alison, fully dressed appeared bearing cups of tea.

'M and D – these are for you. The boys are clean, fed and on their way to rugby practice. I'll see you later. I'm meeting Minnie – we're going to do some revision together.'

And she kissed each of them on the head before leaving the room. Dan and Anna looked at each other, grinned and drank their tea.

'I have a strong feeling that things are righting themselves. Improving actually – look at Alison. Amazing! Thank goodness it's Saturday. We can chill a little.' Dan stretched, got out of bed and moving towards the dressing table bent his head forward, shook his hair and brushed it. He had done this every day since he and Anna had lived together – and no doubt long before. He then tied the pony tail and returned to his bed and the cup of tea.

'I guess we need to get hold of Nancy and I'll probably have to go to the police station – answer questions and so on?'

'I guess so. We might also find things out too – don't you think?'

'Bloody hope so.'

They showered, had breakfast with two pots of coffee before heading again into London and the police station near Waterloo. When they arrived they waited in the foyer by the front desk operated once again by the rather self-effacing, vague woman who had taken charge of Anna's possessions when she had been cautioned.

So long ago!

'I believe Dr. Strong will want to take you up to her office. She's busy at the minute but she'll come to fetch you soon.'

They smiled and nodded their thanks. And then they settled down to wait. It was too quiet to talk. Strange for a central London police station Anna thought but she was grateful for the stillness. She turned her thoughts to Donald Delaney and what was happening with him now.

He was my friend. I truly believed it. And Sandy – he tried to look after me. He knew things and he knew more about Donald than I ever did. Did Donald kill Ellie? Truly?

She and Dan remained in the reception area for what seemed like ages. In fact it was nearly an hour but neither seemed to mind. They were in a stupor – a pleasant one right now. Anna pondered on the drama of the past couple of days. Attacked twice – she winced as she recalled the bruises and the sore skin where Donald had bound her.

Could Donald reveal who had attacked her at Ellie's house?

She thought she knew something about why Ben had been so hostile and the reason that Ellie had apparently hated her. It had not always been so. Ellie and Anna had been true friends. Donald had told Ellie lies. Anna knew now just how envious and destructive Donald could be – and all about something as pointless as who was chosen for a committee role, or who was promoted first.

Then Nancy appeared, beckoning to Anna and Dan to follow her. They nodded to the woman at the desk and followed Nancy up the stairs and along the now familiar corridor to her office. All 3 moved in silence. Their mood felt sombre but Anna could discern a sense of hopefulness too.

'Come and sit down. I've even made a pot of coffee!' Nancy beamed at them and the atmosphere immediately became more relaxed. Anna sensed a freedom that had escaped her in recent days. Nancy looked at them wearing a broad smile on her face. Anna was surprised.

Is there anything to be so happy about?

'I have some news. Some loose ends tied up.' Nancy looked pleased with herself and both Anna and Dan considered it well deserved. Nancy poured them both a coffee, then one for herself. Anna looked at Nancy in anticipation.

'So - a complicated tale has woven itself around you and the Psychology Department as USEL.'

Firstly, I want to report that Donald Delaney has been

charged with both Ellie Hart's murder and as an accessory to the murder of Simon Heath.'

Anna gulped.

'How could he? Ellie? We both loved her. She was gentle, generous .... But that has nothing to do with it does it?'

'I know how upsetting this must be for you love. But as the saying goes – it has all come out in the wash – and I wanted the two of you to know. And as you will see you have both contributed to solving serious crimes.'

'Really? How?'

'Patience my dear. Drink your coffee and let me enjoy this part – the revelations. Donald Delaney has coughed to quite a lot – trying to save his skin. He knows a great deal about other people's fears and transgressions - and he is involved with them. Believe me.'

Dan smiled. Anna stared at Nancy and gulped down some more coffee. She had a feeling of disbelief about the whole drama. Nancy's pleasure at divulging some of what had happened reinforced the sense of make-believe.

The second matter to report – Delaney told Ellie Hart that you had actively blocked her promotion to a personal chair – professorship.'

'How and why would I do that? I think she is ... was great. A chair was late in coming.'

'I expect that is how she must have felt. Totally confused' Dan proposed. 'No wonder she came to hate you – particularly because you must have behaved as if you would never do anything to harm her .....'

'Which I never would.'

'Of course – but imagine how she felt. Donald, your mutual friend, quietly informing her of your treachery. You – oblivious – but to her – you were behaving as if there was nothing in the world you wouldn't do to help her.'

Anna wanted to be sick. She also wanted to scream. But it was too late.

'Poor Ellie probably died still believing that of me.' Anna

found it difficult to think about that possibility.

'But maybe … well perhaps when he killed her - he told her something?' Nancy tried to comfort Anna.

'I also need to tell you that it was Ellie who ransacked your office – she believed you had a copy of a letter to the old VC – Adrian Hanlon – discussing her lack of merit. She found nothing and tried again which is when Delaney found her there and killed her.'

'Why was he there?' Anna's voice was squeaky at that point. Nancy shook her head.

'It's not clear. He claims he was looking for you and thought she had been tampering with your personal possessions but ….. he's sticking to that story - but I can hardly believe him.'

'Can you go on please Nancy?' Dan urged.

'Of course – I've lost count now of which point I'm raising. So now - some of the other plot twists and players. Simon Heath's murder. That was the result of complex interwoven lives.'

'What do you mean?'

'You'll see! Now one of you told me that Heath, Hanlon, this man 'Jim' and Joanna Pearce had all worked at the University of Littlehampton at some point in the not too distant past.'

'True. We found that on the internet.'

'Well it turns out – at least it all fits – that Joana Pearce had had an affair with Heath.'

'You're kidding? Yuk.'

'No, it's true. In fact Dorothy has her – Pearce - in custody now.'

'Christ.'

'Ok. Now Joanna Pearce was told by Adrian Hanlon – who by the way absolutely loathed Heath – well it seems that Hanlon had discovered that Heath was writing memoirs. In other words – a tell-tale of his sexual adventures. He was going to name Shirley Collins and Joanna Pearce among others. You of course I'm afraid. So Hanlon told Pearce it seems.'

'My God then when I told her about Heath …. Doing that to

me. God. I get it now. At least I am beginning to understand something.'

Anna paused: 'But then who killed Heath? That was a very bloody murder – you said it had to be the work of a man. But the style seemed like a sort of revenge.'

'I am not certain as yet but from what I have learned – I was watching Dorothy and Raymond interviewing Pearce – I think that Jim McMullen – that's his real name. Well she got him to kill Heath.'

'Why would he?'

'Money. She paid him. I'm afraid she hated you too – well especially after you told her about you and Heath.'

'But this man Jim – he used Heath's email to contact me – even after Heath was dead. How?

'Because of her HR role at Littlehampton – she was able to clone Heath's phone and his email. Well it was hardly necessary anyway as there was no mobile on his body – so it is likely that he used the genuine mobile to contact you.'

'So - Jim was able to pretend to be him ... on email too?'

'Apparently yes.'

'But what about Ben Hart? She didn't know him. How did she get to his phone?'

'Well it turns out that Delaney found Ben's number on Ellie's phone and Pearce was able to pretend to be him – essentially to lure you to his house and frighten you.'

'I *was* frightened.'

'And to add to this mix Delaney was blackmailing Pearce. Heath had told Delaney sometime in the recent past about Joanna Pearce. Delaney told Shirley Collins out of spite and .... Well ....'

'This is a lot for Anna – well for both of us - to take in Nancy.'

'And for me – don't forget most crimes of this type are more straightforward. Sex or love or money. I suppose fear and rivalry too – there is a little of that. But even so most people would find it hard to believe what some aspects of university life can be like. Forget the peaceful, quiet ivory tower.'

'Too bloody true.'

'And don't forget you two – I knew Donald Delaney as a fellow criminologist. I have been pretty bloody shocked by all of this.'

Anna grabbed Nancy's arm.

'Of course. And if it hadn't been for you ...'

'To go on a little further with the puzzle of Jim.'

'Ok. You mean what he told me about Dan killing his mother?'

'The same. It seems you had told Ellie about what you had discovered of Dan's past – the doctor bit and the woman run over - anyway. And then of course she told Delaney just as she would. Well of course Delaney – the man we know now - stored the information away. When the time was right he told Joanna Pearce – at the end of the last summer term.'

'Why then? We were still apparently all friends then.'

'Not really.'

'I know that now of course but still not clear .....,'

'It seems, from Delaney anyway, that he had been worried about your state of health and suggested to Pearce that you were concerned about your husband's past life and the Sheffield story and so on. You can guess how it went now can't you?'

Anna felt totally downcast. 'Yes. I guess.'

'Don't feel down darling' Dan grabbed Anna's hand and squeezed it. 'It's over now.'

'Well it seems to me that Pearce seized on the idea to get at you, reduce your confidence in the hope that you might leave USEL. She wanted you out of the way. As I understand it from talking to Delaney – simply because your presence reminded her that Heath was not the romantic hero she had thought him to be.'

All three went quiet. Anna thought of how difficult it was to trust anyone. Even Dan the man she cared so much for. But now at least it appeared that there was a glimmer of truth on the near horizon. And I know too that I had lied about who I was. Can we all begin again?

EPILOGUE

As the train left Endlesham on its way to Waterloo Anna reflected on the events of last year.

What was worse – finding out the person you thought was a close friend had been your undercover enemy or not knowing that he was?

If you don't know, can it hurt you?

Well of course it *did* hurt her. There was so much she had been unable to make sense of – Gabriel and John Jones avoiding her. Ellie and her soft rejection of Anna's friendship. Donald and Shirley? He had told her so many untruths that his relationship with Shirley – the woman he had always claimed to hate – was almost of no consequence now. Poor Shirley. Anna even felt a strange surge of pity for a brief moment.

How could any of them have believed the poison they were fed?

Anna tried too to understand how she had been so lacking in insight and self-preserving instinct as to confide in Joanna Pearce about the rape.

Well she did betray herself by informing the police that I was making an allegation against Simon Heath. But I didn't get it then. It was just something else that was annoying, humiliating and that didn't fit my picture of what Joanna was like. Nor did it make sense in terms of HR protocol.

Perhaps, she thought, the only person I was right to trust was Sandy.

He did look after my interests. He did seem to care that I wasn't undermined. But he never told me that Michael had seen what Simon did to me. And how terrible that turned out to be for Michael. And was it my fault that Michelle was also raped? And maybe even murdered? I'll never know but I can't forget.

And most of all Anna felt guilty that she had believed the toxic account of Dan's life that Jim had presented. But then her thoughts moved to Dan. He had never been the person she thought she knew. And she wondered how far, after all that had happened to both of them, the truth had emerged.

What kind of creature is he really?

She loved him. On a day-to-day basis he was a great husband and father. He cared for her. Or appeared to. There is no doubting that he loved and looked after the children. But what else might there be to know? And ultimately did it matter? Maybe all that really counts is how someone behaves.

She suddenly noticed that Gabriel Watson was sitting a few seats in front of her.

The poor man. He had been a good head of department, but he fell apart following the arrest and sentencing of Donald Delaney. He had been called as a character witness and had supported Donald. But in so doing he had lost the confidence of Ian Fielding who had by then been confirmed as VC. She wondered if Gabriel would ever recover from the humiliation he experienced after the full story had emerged.

He's a psychologist but he failed to understand the politics and the deceit. I don't blame him – well not totally. But he didn't give me the benefit of the doubt.

Soon after Delaney's trial and imprisonment, Fielding promoted Anna who was now the head of department while Gabriel was side-lined as assistant postgraduate tutor to the woman he really had hated – Shirley Collins. She had already raised a complaint against him suggesting he failed to support Black and ethnic minority students against discrimination.

* * *

PRAISE FOR AUTHOR

'Not normally my kind of book but I loved it .... keeping you intrigued'

'I loved the book a real page turner'

- CONTAINMENT: A NOVEL

'A must read for dads, grandparents and anyone in the caring professions'

'Paula Nicolson manages to inspire'

*- POSTNATAL DEPRESSION: FACING THE PARADOX OF LOVE, LOSS
AND MOTHERHOOD*

'Not a book for light reading but I have found it very useful'

- DOMESTIC VIOLENCE AND PSYCHOLOGY

BOOKS BY THIS AUTHOR

Containment: A Novel

A Wilson Coffey Spy story

Genealogy, Psychology And Identity

How far does knowledge of your own family history impact on your sense of identity? Does it help you understand yourself?

Domestic Violence And Psychology

A review of research on domestic violence and abuse particularly examining the role of psychological practice

Postnatal Depression: Facing The Paradox Of Loss

Exploring women's experiences of depression after childbirth

A Critical Approach To Human Growth And Development

Case studies and theory for understanding social and emotional aspects of human development

ACKNOWLEDGEMENTS

As ever I want to thank my friends, colleagues and family for love and support for all my writing.